DEATH BY BEER

A WIZARD DETECTIVE PARANORMAL ROMANCE

KARIN DE HAVIN

THE WIZARD DETECTIVE DERRICK DUNNE SERIES

Death by Swordfish book four and the final book in the series is coming early next year!

The Shifter Vampire Alliance Serial

The Shifter Vampire Alliance features Derrick Dunne and takes place in the same world as The Wizard Detective Series.

Episodes 1-7 are complete and ready to take you on a paranormal adventure!

****The Witching World of Avalon** features Derrick Dunne and takes place in the same world as The Wizard Detective Series.**

Join Karin's newsletter for book inspired recipes in the *Baking with Books* segment and receive a free short story!

Click here to join Karin's newsletter!

KARIN'S SERIES

**Indicates FINISHED series **

If you like Harry Potter with genies, read...

The Genie Academy**

If you like Twilight with wizards, read...

The Girl Chameleon**

If you like The Hunger Games set in Heaven, read...

Nine Lives Part One**

If you like Buffy the Vampire Slayer, read...

How to Snag a Shifter**

If you like books set in foreign lands with ghosts, read...

Tokyo Academy-First Contact**

If you like happily ever after time travel romances, read...

Jin In Time Part One**

If you like books that take place in the world of celebrities and fashion with a fantasy twist, read...

Celebrity Witch**

Copyright © 2022 by Karin De Havin

Published by 9 Yards Publishing

Edited by Lily Luchesi

Cover design by Storm Jensen

All rights reserved

This book is the property of Karin De Havin, in all media both physical and digital. No one, except the owner of this property, may reproduce, copy or publish in any medium any of this book without the expressed permission of the author of this work.

This is a work of fiction. The characters, places, brands, and events portrayed in this book are products of the author's imagination. Any similarity to real persons, living or dead, is coincidental and not intended by the author.

No part of this book may be reproduced or stored in a retrieval system or transmitted in any form or by any means, electronic, mechanical, photocopying, recording, or otherwise without express written permission of the author. This eBook is licensed for your enjoyment only. It may not be re-sold or given away to other people.

To Dave: Who can deduce I need a snack to keep writing better than anyone!

To Sammy: You are the cutest sidekick until you bring me a lizard tail.

To Storm: My very own book dragon who thought Derrick deserved his very own series. You were right!

1

DYNAMIC DUO

Running my hand over my beloved Beemer sedan's steering wheel, I knew I was truly back home. The endless rows of tall palm trees dotting the skyline were also a big clue.

Fiona squeezes my shoulder. "Do you need some alone time?"

I chuckled. "Maybe later." I click the key and the trunk pops open. "First we need to get to my bungalow. Mr. Kumar texted me that he transported Holmes there. I don't want him thinking I've abandoned him."

Fiona tucks her luggage in the back carefully and I realize she hasn't brought her homing pigeon, Shiva, with her. She leans back in the passenger seat and stretches out her long legs. "It's nice to be back in the sunshine state."

I laugh. "The weather is considerably better than London."

"I wholeheartedly agree with you."

As I change lanes my curiosity gets the better of me. "Can I ask why you didn't bring Shiva with you?"

She lets out a deep sigh. "I wanted to bring her along, but it wouldn't be fair. Her homing instinct is for London. She's in good hands. I gave her to my mum. She loves birds. Shiva will be spoiled rotten, just like my mum's three parakeets."

"I think Shiva will enjoy her retirement." I sit back, enjoying the familiar purr of the engine.

Fiona squeezes my hand resting on the console. "How can I ever compete with your Beemer?"

I lean over and kiss her cheek. "You have nothing to worry about. You're my number one woman."

She laughs as I pull out of the parking garage and I head away from the airport and onto the 405 freeway towards Santa Monica and home.

Fiona moves her seat back a bit and takes in the endless city skyline of Los Angeles. "I never thought I'd come back to Los Angeles so soon." She gives me a sly smile. "Are you sure you didn't cast a spell on me?"

I return the smile with one of my own. "The only spell I cast on you was my charm."

She reaches out and runs her finger along my jawline. "I must admit they are pretty irresistible."

My smile fades as quickly as the traffic on the freeway turns bumper to bumper. "All joking aside, I have to admit I'm still in shock you are sitting next to me. For you to request a job transfer to Los Angeles blew me away."

Fiona looked out the window. "Working with you again made me realize there was no point in trying to keep you at arm's length. We make great partners, and I could feel your charms working their way into my heart."

Something I hoped for but chose not to push. Either she found me attractive, or she didn't. Noah, her former partner and boyfriend, looks like a Swedish model. I'm the complete opposite. Dark hair and eyes and a distinctive mysterious yet sexy look. At least that's what Jennifer and other women have said about me. Thankfully Fiona doesn't have a type. I do. Fiona is so very much like Tara. Tall, beautiful, and powerful.

Fiona touches the top of my hand. "Penny for your thoughts?"

"I was thinking about the first time we met. You took my breath away with your stunning beauty. I thought you were totally out of my league."

Her cheeks flush. "I thought the same thing once I found out you were a wizard of the Twelfth Order. Everyone in the paranormal world knows how powerful your magic is."

I give her a wicked smile. "I see; so it had nothing to do with my looks or my charm. It was all about my powerful magic."

She punches me in the bicep just as I had seen Jennifer do to Ainsley. Something I thought was so cute until now. I take my hand off the wheel for a second and rub the spot where she hit me. "You pack a punch, literally."

"It's from growing up with brothers. I had to learn to defend myself early on."

"Do you think they would approve of me?"

She smiles. "They are a tough bunch when it comes to protecting my honor, but I think you'd be able to win them over, eventually."

I knew it was a bit premature to be talking about meeting her family, but I truly hoped we would reach that point in the future. Fiona looks out at the palm trees that dot the landscape as we get off the freeway and head toward my bungalow.

She rolls down the window and breathes in the air. "There is still a bit of the smoggy city smell, but also I catch a hint of the salt of the ocean. I can understand why you wanted to live in Santa Monica."

"Yes, I wanted to get as close to the beach as possible. Not because I'm some secret surfer, but because of the salt in the air. Also, it's so much cooler here. The only downside is the fog. But anywhere you live has tradeoffs. Even Tahiti."

Fiona chuckles. "I don't know, but Tahiti sounds pretty good to me." She eyes my arms. "I still think you might be a secret surfer. Those biceps of yours look like they aren't from time at the gym."

She is right about that. I did have a secret sport—beach volleyball. But I wanted it to be a surprise. "Men like to have a bit of mystery."

As I turn down my street, my heart skips a beat. Every time I see my little Craftsman bungalow after being away it has the same reaction. It misses home.

I park the Beemer in the driveway, get the bags out of the trunk and am greeted by the bellowing sound of Holmes's bark greets me.

Turning the key, I open the door to an ambush.

Holmes stands up on his hindquarters and slobbers all over my face. "I'm so glad you are home."

Then he jumps down to face Fiona clutching her roller bag. "What are you doing here? Did you stow away on Derrick's flight back to Los Angeles?"

Fiona chuckles. "Good to see you too Holmes. As a matter of fact, I transferred to the Los Angeles division of WI-6."

Holmes turns his back on us and trots back into the house.

Fiona whispers in my ear. "That went well."

I kissed her on the cheek. "He'll get over it. He really does like you."

We pull our bags into the living room only to face Holmes once again. This time he is scowling in front of his doggie bed. "She is not going to live here, is she?"

Holmes is acting like a jealous ex-girlfriend. "I'm disappointed in your behavior, Holmes. Fiona is a colleague and a friend, and you will treat her as such."

My stern voice has the desired effect. Holmes's rigid posture relaxes a bit. He looks up at Fiona. "I must apologize for my harsh words."

She walks over and pats him on his massive head and strokes one of his long floppy ears. "Apology accepted. I didn't mean to invade your turf. Rest assured as soon as I can find a place to live, I will no longer violate your decidedly male space."

I chuckle. "I admit I've been known to leave a sweaty sock or two around the house." Pointing to my bedroom, I snap my fingers to tidy up the decidedly messy room I left behind before I flew off to London. "My room is now stinky sock and underwear free. There are clean sheets on the bed and clean towels in the bathroom. My casa is yours as long as you need it."

Fiona goes to reach out for me but pulls her hand back when Holmes glowers at her. "Thank you. I will look for a flat tomorrow. I'm hoping I can afford a flat by the beach as well."

"I think that should be no problem. Rent in one of the apartment buildings just two blocks away is cheaper than the flats at Primrose Hill."

Fiona plops down on my leather sofa. "That's a relief because I thought oceanfront property costs a fortune."

Holmes cuts in. "If you wanted to purchase a home, but renting, although high, is still somewhat affordable, especially compared to London's popular neighborhoods."

Fiona cracks a smile. "Holmes, I had no idea you were interested in real estate."

I sit down next to Fiona making sure to leave a bit of cushion space between us. "She's right. Have you been taking courses at night?"

Holmes snorts. "Don't be silly. But I do like to

watch TV when I'm left alone. I find the *Agents of Sunset* quite amusing."

Who knew Holmes watches TV? He must turn it off when I come home. "Ah, so you have a guilty pleasure."

Holmes's doggie brow furrows. "Guilty of what?"

Fiona chuckles as she stands back up. "It is an American expression. It means you are watching a program with little or no redeeming qualities. Like a soap opera."

Holmes continues to be confused. "But I learned quite a lot about real estate transactions from *Million Dollar Listing*. I think I could easily aid Derrick if he wished to purchase a home."

"I'm sure you could." Fiona pulls her bag toward the hallway covering up a yawn as she holds onto the roller bag with the other hand. "If you don't mind, I'm going to go to bed. The time difference is hitting me hard."

I get up and roll Fiona's bag into my bedroom. "Make yourself at home. I'll conjure a bed like I did in my London flat when Jennifer was visiting."

Fiona kisses me on the cheek, her eyes showing how fatigued she is. "I'm sorry but I must check out."

British slang is so amusing. "Good night." I return her kiss and close the door.

As soon as I make it back into the living room Holmes blocks my path. "Something has changed between you two. You are more intimate with one another. Did you mate?"

Again, he brings up his obsession with mating. "It's

none of your business, but no. We did kiss and hug, however. And you are going to have to get used to us becoming a couple."

Holmes stares up at me with the look of defeat in his eyes. "I knew it would happen. It's obvious you are attracted to her. I suppose I should be happy for you, but I worry we will spend even less time together."

I hang my head knowing I have neglected him terribly yet again. "I'm sorry, Holmes. And I promise since we are back in Los Angeles, we will take you with us on our cases."

He eyes the bedroom. "You aren't going to sneak in there while I am asleep, are you?"

I cross my heart. "I am a gentleman.

Holmes exhales hard enough that I can smell his doggie breath. "Good." He eyes his bed. "I'm tired. Night."

I snap my fingers and the same single bed I conjured when Jennifer visited my London flat replaces my leather sofa.

Snapping my fingers again, I conjure a glass full of sleeping potion and change into my pajama bottoms. I am still reeling from the fact that Fiona cares enough about me that she requested to be transferred to Los Angeles.

Sitting on the edge of the bed, I down the potion and then climb under the covers. My eyes shut and I doze off, dreaming of a life with Fiona.

8

A BEAM OF SUNLIGHT STREAMS THROUGH THE WOOD blinds, causing my eyelids to flutter open. I gaze around and find Holmes snoring away in his velvet doggie bed and Fiona isn't up yet. I have a few solitary moments to myself. Something I haven't had in months. I put my arms under my head and stare up at the ceiling. Ah, to have the free time to do something as mundane as count the specs of dust on the living room light fixture. I flash back to the day I bought the vintage fixture at an antique store on La Brea. I thought the reverse painted fall leaves on the glass panes matched the Craftsman décor of the bungalow perfectly. After five minutes I'm so zoned out I don't hear Fiona come into the room.

"What is so fascinating about your light fixture? It does have a nice vintage design and the combination of oranges and reds of the leaves are quite pleasant, but I must say it could use a good cleaning."

I chuckle and sit up forgetting I have no pajama top on. "I let my housekeeper go when I got the job in London."

Fiona eyes my exposed chest. "It seems you have the time to work out. Impressive abdominal muscles."

Holmes bolts up right out of his bed. "Derrick, cover yourself."

Fiona bursts out laughing. "Holmes fancies himself back in Victorian England."

"That he does." I snap my fingers and a matching green and blue plaid pajama top covers my offending chest. I glare down at the black and tan mass next to me. "Holmes you can be so prudish. Half the time you sound like my grandmother."

He huffs. "I am just looking out for you. That is all."

Fiona moves over to Holmes. "How about a nice walk along the beach after breakfast? Does that sound good, Holmes?"

I bet Fiona broke up many a fight between her brothers. She handled the tension between Holmes and I like a champ.

Holmes steps out of his doggie bed. "I think that sounds like a splendid idea." He gazes over at me. "A little sea air sounds like the perfect remedy. Hopefully it will improve a certain someone's mood."

"What do you want me to conjure for breakfast?"

Holmes perks up. "I would like one of those marvelous blood sausages."

I make barfing noises and Fiona laughs. "And for the lady?"

Fiona catches her breath. "I'm a bit jet lagged so I'm not terribly hungry. I think a fruit cup and a yogurt will do the trick."

I snap my fingers and the blood sausage materializes at Holmes's feet. Snapping them again, Fiona's fruit cup and yogurt materialize on the dining room table. With them handled, I try to think what I would like for breakfast. Always rushing for time, I usually make a protein shake and run out the door. Today I want to linger just a bit with Fiona over breakfast. My gut tells me alone time with her will be precious in the future. I snap my fingers and two eggs over easy, a piece of avocado toast, and a glass of orange juice materialize across from Fiona.

I sit down as Fiona eyes my avocado toast. "I can think of anything more Californian than avocado smashed on toast."

I give her a smile. "Are you a bit jealous?"

She chuckles. "Maybe."

I hold my hand up getting ready to snap my fingers, but she wraps her hand around mine. "Thank you, but I need to not overindulge."

I take in Fiona's trim figure. "Really? I would think you can eat whatever you want, just like me."

"If I had time to work out, but I never do as a detective. It's a pretty sedentary job."

She's right. We are either driving somewhere, in the office doing paperwork, or interviewing suspects and witnesses. "You've got a point. Doing reconnaissance, I did a lot of driving, but I also had a fair amount of legwork."

Holmes trots next to me. "Can I have another sausage before we go for a walk?"

I pat him on the head. "Ok. But let's not make a habit of it. Mr. Bullock made you, so you didn't need to eat. I think I've spoiled you a bit too much with the treats. You want to eat as much as a regular dog."

He nudges me with his nose and looks up at me with those big, sad brown eyes. "But food tastes so good."

I snap my fingers and a blood sausage drops next to

his paws. "Fine. But understand I'm not going to bend to your food whims like I did in London."

Holmes totally ignores me as he practically swallows the blood sausage whole.

Fiona smiles knowingly. "You don't need any children with Holmes around."

Is she trying to let me know she isn't interested in kids? I haven't really thought about having any since Tara and I were engaged. I look over at Holmes and know I can barely handle taking care of a dog.

I give her a knowing smile. "He sure is."

Holmes lets out a loud bark. "I can hear you."

Fiona goes over and pets him on the head. "Sorry, Holmes." She gives me a wink. "You're a good boy most of the time." She gazes at the door and then looks down at her purple robe. "Let me get dressed and we can go for that walk I promised."

"That would be marvelous." Holmes glares at my pajama-clad body. "I think you need to do the same, Derrick."

My job is a lot easier than Fiona's, I think to myself as I snap my fingers and my pajamas are replaced by a pair of black trousers and a black and gray striped shirt. It's my de facto WI-6 uniform. I smile when Fiona emerges from the bathroom in record time wearing one of her pantsuits. This time it is a pretty navy blue with a white silk blouse underneath.

She strides over to the strip of hooks I have one the wall behind the door and pulls off Holmes's leash. "Okay boy. Let's get some brisk sea air."

Holmes bounds over next to Fiona, and she snaps the leash on his collar. "You ready, Derrick?"

"Sure, let me snag my keys and we'll be off." Grabbing my keys off the side table, I'm about to head out the door to join them when a viewing screen pops up over my dining room-slash-office table. I swallow hard when I see that the usually smiling face of Mr. Kumar is a stern one. "Good morning, sir."

He does a sideways glance and sees Fiona and Holmes by the front door. "Am I interrupting something?"

Fiona gives me a wink and leads Holmes out the door and closes it behind her. "No, sir. Fiona is just taking Holmes out for his morning walk before we head over to WI-6."

"Glad to see you are all getting along so well. This won't take long." He eyes the small single bed I conjured for myself sitting in the background. "It appears you are not getting paid enough by WI-6. At least you could conjure yourself a sleeper sofa. It would be more practical."

Mr. Kumar, always the problem solver. "That is an excellent idea, sir." I snap my fingers and the single bed is seamlessly replaced by a Craftsman inspired leather sleeper sofa.

Mr. Kumar gives me a light applause. "Your conjuring magic continues to improve. Nicely done."

"Thank you, sir. And thank you for the sleeper sofa suggestion. It may take a few days for Ms. Singh to find a place of her own."

A faint smile crosses his lips. "I hope you are pleased with her joining the WI-6 Los Angeles detective staff."

I try not to broadcast just how pleased I am. "Yes, I'm glad she has moved to Los Angeles. I think we work well together."

There is a twinkle in his eyes. "I think you have a chemistry on several levels."

Did the Order spy on my flight back home? I wouldn't put it past them. "Sir, I can assure you we are consummate professionals and will keep our budding relationship quiet."

He nods. "Good, because we wouldn't want Mr. Pierre to get wind of it. He would find a way to turn the relationship to his advantage."

I know he's right. "We will be sure to fake a few arguments every once and awhile."

He chuckles. "From what I hear, you won't have to fake that part of your relationship."

The hairs on the back of my neck bristle. The Order seems way too invested in my relationship with Fiona. Could our budding romance have been created by magic?"

"Derrick, please understand we want the best for all our wizards. Your grief for Tara has gone on far longer than we thought was healthy. But we would never use magic when it comes to love matches. That is the work of witches and cupids."

I want to let out a huge sigh of relief, but I keep myself under control. Mr. Kumar is never one for chitchat. There is a reason why he wants to talk to me. "That is good to hear. How can I help you, sir?"

"I have a special request for you. One you are uniquely qualified for."

My mouth goes dry. The last time I heard those words from his lips I almost died. "Anything I can do to help the Twelfth Order."

"We need you to go back to Zoomer driving at night. Just for a little while. We have a renegade paranormal who is stirring up a bit of trouble. He has managed to dodge us so far."

Only the most powerful of paranormals can evade the Order. "Alright, sir. Can you tell me who I will be trying to find?"

"Of course. A demigod. One I believe you have met before."

2

THE UNUSUAL DEATH SQUAD

My mind reels with the news from Mr. Kumar. The only demigod I know is Tad Ryan, the A-lister movie star. Why would he go rogue?

No, it can't be him. But I can't remember meeting another one off the top of my head. While I rack my brain, running through the endless paranormals I've met, Fiona comes strolling through the door, looking a bit worse for wear from her beach walk with Holmes. Her normally slick black hair is full of tangles, and she has sand in her sneakers.

She frowns at me. "What happened to you coming along for our walk?"

Holmes looks up at me and shakes his head. "Sometimes I wonder who you really work for. The Order or WI-6."

I sigh. "Both. The Order wants me to resume my Zoomer duties at night."

Holmes stomps his front paw. "That is asking too much. You will have no energy left for WI-6 during the day."

It's as if Holmes is speaking for his creator, my WI-6 Los Angeles boss, Mr. Bullock.

Fiona takes off Holmes's leash and hangs it up on one of the hooks behind the door. "Holmes has point."

"If I was a regular person, I would agree, but I am a wizard."

Holmes takes three big gulps of water from his bowl and then turns to face me. "I don't think it is right."

Once again Fiona steps in to mediate. "I trust Derrick's judgment. If he says he can do both jobs equally well, then I support him."

Holmes mutters under his breath, "Figures."

Fiona ignores his snide remark. "I'm going to freshen up and then let's head out to WI-6."

I nod knowing we need to be at the office at nine o'clock and she wants to look her best. "Sounds good."

He barks in protest. "You aren't taking me with you?"

"I'm sorry, but we have a ton of paperwork to fill out left over from our case in London. It's a catch-up day and you would be bored to death."

Fiona joins us looking as if she hadn't spent an hour on the beach. Her make-up and hair are flawless. "I promise he is telling the truth, Holmes. We left London in a hurry."

His doggie brow furrows. "Exactly." He eye's Fiona. "What was the rush?"

"When the Order and WI-6 say it's time to return home you don't argue."

He huffs. "Fine. But this better be the only time I'm left home alone."

I grab my car keys and Fiona grabs her Bayberry purse. We say in unison, "We promise," then rush out the door as fast as we can.

Once we are in the car and driving down the 405 freeway, we breathe a sigh of relief. Fiona turns to me and chuckles. "A certain canine sure got up on the wrong side of the doggie bed this morning."

Guilt keeps me from laughing. "I did promised to take him with us when we are working."

The screen flickers signaling a text message is coming in. "What now?" I say as the hands-free system kicks in and reads me the message. *"This is Scott. Just a heads up that after you have your meeting with Mr. Bullock you will be headed to The Pit, where you will be greeted by two new detectives. Oh, and Mr. Bullock has a surprise for Ms. Singh to welcome her to the Los Angeles division. See you soon."*

Fiona puts her hand on her chin like the famous sculpture *The Thinker* by Rodin. "I wonder what my surprise is going to be. Maybe an apartment by the ocean."

I chuckle. "I highly doubt that. He might give you what he gave me."

Her face lights up. "A BMW?"

I stroke the leather steering wheel. "That was a gift from the Order, remember?"

She gives my shoulder a squeeze. "I was just teasing. But what was the gift Mr. Bullock gave you?"

"A primo parking spot right up front in the parking garage. It ticked Smith and Ross off big time. They had to earn theirs. Oh, and a gift basket full of detective novels."

Fiona makes a pouty face like a two-year-old. "You have to be kidding about the novels. And what good is a parking spot when I don't have a car?"

"That can be remedied." I hold out my hand. "I can conjure whatever you want. Would you like a Rover like you had in London?"

She bats her long lush eyelashes. "You know the way to a girl's heart. Dating a wizard is going to be amazing."

I chuckle. "Now don't get any *Housewives of Beverly Hills* ideas."

We laugh all the way down the off ramp onto Spring Street. She squeezes my hand resting on the console. "I promise I won't be high maintenance like a celebrity."

Something I know she could never be. "I'm going to hold you to that."

⁊

Fiona's eyes light up taking in her surprise. "I can't believe I get my own dog."

Mr. Bullock beams. "At first I thought I would

conjure you an Afghan. They are elegant and sleek. A perfect match for you. But then I thought better of it. You are those things, but you are also bright and clever. Standard Poodles have brains to spare."

As I take in the poodle's silky black fur and the perfect modern cut where most of the body is clipped close. Unlike the more traditional cuts, this one only has a slight poof at the very top of the head like a hat. I secretly wonder if Mr. Bullock is giving Fiona a Standard Poodle to tick off Mr. Pierre. His precious Fifi with her white fur and exaggerated pom pom cut will have some competition.

Stroking the poodle's head, Fiona asks, "Do you have a name for her?"

"Yes, I thought Renoir would be an appropriate name. In homage to the famous painter, but also for the female detective in the popular TV series in France."

Fiona claps her hands together. "I love it. Renoir it is."

I can but help wonder if the name is also to tick off Mr. Pierre.

The poodle barks its approval and then says in French accented English, "It will be my pleasure to serve you, Ms. Singh."

She tucks the poodle under its long muzzle. "Please call me Fiona."

I watch the two of them together and think they make such a perfect pair. Holmes and I on the other hand are like the odd couple.

Scott motions for us to head toward the door. "It's time to meet the new crew in *The Pit*."

Fiona nods and turns back to face Mr. Bullock, but he has vanished. More than likely he's off to another meeting.

Fiona says to Scott, "Please tell Mr. Bullock thank you for my gift."

Scott straightens his pale turquoise colored suit jacket and opens the door for her and Renoir. "He already knows by your reaction."

I watch as the poodle struts gracefully out into the lobby and know I'm going to have a lovesick Holmes on my hands. I'm going to have to give him a fatherly lecture on how Renoir is off limits. Of course, he won't take me seriously now that Fiona and I are a couple. Maybe I should cast a protective barrier around her when Holmes is around. Knowing Holmes's infatuation with poodles, it will be a must.

Scott claps his hands and in a loud voice says, "Mr. Dunne, are you coming with us?"

I speedwalk over to the elevator, totally embarrassed. "Yes, of course. I can't wait to see the new gang, and most of all Mr. Pierre."

Scott smiles showing off his brilliant white teeth. "Talk about laying on the sarcasm." He pushes the button to the 30th floor, the home of *The Pit*.

Fiona strokes Renoir's poof ball on her head. "Gird your loins."

I burst out laughing along with Scott. His perfectly styled hair doesn't move an inch despite how hard he is laughing. "Fiona has the right attitude to survive *The Pit.*"

I wish I could say the same. For me there is nothing to laugh about. Poor Mr. Davies was impaled on an umbrella because of me. At least Smith thought to chloroform him, or his death would have been agony. "I don't know how I will be able to hold myself back from strangling Mr. Pierre."

"You have no choice," comes Scott's voice in my head. For a moment I'd forgotten he was a fellow wizard and wasn't just Mr. Bullock's flamboyant executive assistant.

The elevator door opens, and Scott hangs back. "Good luck you two."

Renoir obediently trots next to Fiona with no clue what she is going to be stepping into. I dart in front of them and open the door. "After you, ladies." When I follow in behind them into *The Pit,* I'm shocked to see the desks laid out in two neat rows. Normally The Pit is so dark I must cast a visual enhancement spell to keep from bumping into things. Has Mr. Pierre decided to change the script?

A familiar face I thought I would never see again greets me with a smile. "Hello Mr. Dunne and Ms. Singh. Good to have you back." Ms. Burke smiles at Fiona in the way only a woman can when a fellow female colleague has put her in her place. "I understand you are permanently joining our team." She looks me up and down and, in a voice, thick with sarcasm she says, "It seems your partner has won you over."

Fiona gives Ms. Burke one of her, I-got-you-fired-I can-do it again smiles. "We are a winning team. Haven't lost a case since we've been together."

Before Ms. Burke can give a fiery retort, Bob Klein, my one-time partner, comes sauntering up next to me. He gives my shoulder a squeeze. "Good to have you back. Where's the snarky Bloodhound of yours?"

I lie, "He's exhausted from his trip back from London."

"Understandable." Bob points proudly to his chocolate lab. "My partner in crime is back by my side." He calls over to a guy who is tending to a bulldog. "Hey, Wayne, come over and meet Derrick."

Wayne must have been named after the old western star since he has that rugged Marlboro Man good looks. Unlike his namesake, he is dressed in a nicely tailored suit that shows off his muscular build. As he comes closer, I can't help but smile when I see he is wearing a pair of expensive snakeskin cowboy boots. He holds out his hand. "Nice to meet you."

He has a distinctive Texas drawl like a western movie star.

Ms. Burke cozies up next to him. "Mr. Thomas is a wonderful addition to our team."

Someone is smitten.

Fiona tells Renoir to heel and then holds out her hand to Wayne. "Nice to meet you. I'm a bit of a newbie to the Los Angeles division as well."

Wayne takes in Fiona's ease and beauty and graces

her with a huge smile. "You're British. You came much further than I did. Across the pond, I think you say."

Fiona nods politely. "Yes. We Brits do lovingly call the Atlantic Ocean a pond."

The distinct smell of mustache wax and mint fills the air as the spitting image of Hercule Poirot enters the room. Mr. Pierre's eyes lock in on mine and in his thick French accent he says, "Enough chit chat with your colleagues; Singh and Dunne, in my office immediately." He turns on his expensive French loafers and strides toward his office as quickly as his short legs will take him.

My fists ball up and part of me wants to turn on my heels and walk straight out of *The Pit* and right back to Twelfth Order Headquarters. Mr. Pierre is going to push my buttons until I either get fired or kill him.

Fiona, sensing my rage, moves behind me and gently pushes me forward. She whispers in my ear, "Keep your cool, Derrick. Don't let the French plonker get to you. Nothing would make him happier than for you to muck something up because of your anger."

I know she's right. Now I wish I'd brought Holmes. He would know how to talk back to Mr. Pierre so I wouldn't be tempted. Instead, it is Fiona who is coming to the rescue. Thank goodness she came with me to Los Angeles. As if we were in a theatrical production, the light suddenly dims in *The Pit* to the point it is extremely hard to see.

Fiona takes a hold of my arm. "Cast a spell so we can find our way to the office."

I cast the visualization spell and the path to Mr. Pierre's office becomes clear. I lead Fiona into the office in time to find Mr. Pierre whispering to someone on his phone.

He looks up with pure hatred in his eyes that only grows stronger as his poodle, Fifi, leaps to her feet at the sight of Renoir. Mr. Pierre hisses at Fiona, "Keep that dog away from my precious Fifi." Then he turns his gaze to me. "I suppose giving Fiona a Standard Poodle was your idea."

If only I had thought of it. When Mr. Bullock said he was giving Fiona a gift I had no idea it would also be an act of revenge. "Sir, can we reestablish our relationship? I'm here to do a good job for WI-6. I have no grudge against you."

My words sound sincere even though I don't mean them.

A hand reaches up to the left-hand side of his pencil thin mustache. "I suppose it would be wise to put the past behind us."

His voice sounds silky smooth. He is lying through his teeth the same way I did.

Fiona, ever the mediator, clears her throat. "Sir, I promise Renoir here," she pats the fluffy black ball on the poodle's head, "will give Fifi the respect of being the senior dog in the division."

I crack a half smile, knowing we've reached a stalemate.

"Glad we made our positions clear." Mr. Pierre waves his hand at us as if we were a pesky insect hovering around his desk. "Don't you have a lot of paperwork to finish?"

We nod and gladly march out the door. I take Fiona's arm and lead her and Renoir back to our desks. It's then I notice the little star statue Mr. Bullock gave me for solving my first case is missing. Knowing Mr. Pierre's hatred of me, it is probably sitting in a giant pile of garbage at the local dump.

Fiona sits down behind her desk and follows my gaze. "Oh no. Your statue is missing. Did you take it home before you left for London?"

Pointing out my obvious misstep would normally get my hackles up but she's only trying to help. I shake my head. "No. In the rush to leave I totally forgot about it." Then another obvious course occurs to me. I snap my fingers and an exact copy of my little star statue once again graces my desk.

She smiles. "Nice move."

Renoir sits regally next to Fiona's desk as her mistress boots up her computer. Fiona digs right in it, filling out her notes on the case of death by umbrella. I, on the other hand, let my mind drift off to my conversation with Mr. Kumar. A demigod is stirring up trouble. I decided to get a bit of a head start on my Zoomer duty tonight by texting someone I thought was a friend and hope still is. I pull out my phone search contacts and message Tad Ryan. He could be on some exotic film location, but I hope I get lucky and catch him between movie projects. *"Hey Tad, long time no talk. Hope you are as awesome as you looked on the cover of Fame. That was quite the tan you were sporting. I hope you know I wouldn't bother you unless it was important, but I'm reaching out for a reason. Respond when you get a chance, thanks, Derrick."*

Fiona eyes me putting my phone back on the desk. "Something up?"

"Just reaching out to a friend I haven't heard from in a while."

She gives me a knowing smile. "Right. I know how much you enjoy filling out reports."

I laugh. "It is a special kind of torture."

My phone buzzes on my desk and I pick it up. It's a text from the former Mr. Sexiest Man Alive. *"Hey, Derrick. You're right it's been too long. I'm on set but headed to my trailer. Give me a buzz."*

I glance around *The Pit* and take in Bob and Wayne going over a case and know it's not safe to talk here. Mr. Pierre has the place bugged and there are surveillance cameras everywhere. I get up and walk over to Fiona's desk. "I've got to get something out of my car I forgot. Can you cover for me?"

She nods looking over at a camera that has zoomed right in on where I'm standing. "No worries."

I chuckle. "I thought you were British, not Aussie."

She tosses a wadded-up piece of paper at me. It bounces off my back as I head toward the door.

Bob picks it up off the floor. "In the doghouse so soon?"

I smile remembering what Mr. Kumar said about Fiona and my reputation for bickering. "Yep."

I look down at my watch. "Only took a half hour of being back working together."

He smiles. "I can understand why you need a break."

I give him a thumbs up and stride out the door. My cover story should give me a good fifteen minutes to talk to Tad. Punching the button to the parking garage, I tap my foot impatiently waiting for the elevator. When it opens, I bite my lip. The head of wizard resources, Mrs. Hardcore, is the last person I want to see.

Wearing her uniform of a black jumpsuit and black high heeled booties, she purses her lips as if she sucked on a lemon. "Mr. Dunne. I have some intake forms I want you and Ms. Singh to fill out." She opens a folder she had tucked under her arm and hands me four pieces of paper. "I need these on my desk today before you leave."

Fantastic. "Can I ask why you didn't email us the forms? We could have printed out a copy."

Mrs. Hardcore's sharp features crinkle forming tiny wrinkles on her pointed nose. "We only want originals at WR. You should know that."

I can feel my time to talk to Tad slipping away like water through a sieve. "Fine."

I push past her as the elevator doors begin to close.

With time ticking away, I race to my car so I can call Tad. The Beemer has a soundproof protective layer covering the entire inside of the car so that my conversations will be safe from the listening devices strategically placed in the parking garage.

As soon as my door is shut, I dial Tad. His famous voice booms from the receiver. "Derrick, how have you been, man? I guess not so good if you are calling me."

I don't laugh. "Actually, I'm good but I'm calling you to let you know one of your demigods has been stirring up enough trouble to show up on the Twelfth Order's radar. And according to Mr. Kumar it's a demigod I have met before."

Dead silence on the other line. Then he sucks in a breath. "Well, besides myself, the only other demigod you might have met is Sebastian. But he is in Indonesia right now so it can't be him."

"Then it is someone impersonating him. A renegade."

Tad taps something small on a hard surface sounding like he's sending out Morse code. "I know you have renegade wizards, but a demigod gone bad is unheard of. My guess it is a shifter at work."

Good thing I'm dating one. Only shifters can recognize each other. "You know what I think you might be right."

Tad's voice sounds less strained. "I'm glad you didn't try to pin it on me. I heard you are a detective now, and I have the perfect alibi."

I chuckle already knowing what his answer is going to be. "Really? What is it?"

"I just came into LA on the red eye. For the last

month I've been shooting a movie in Fiji." He laughs. "I have plenty of witnesses."

He gets to travel to the greatest places for work. "Awesome. Hey, now that you are back in town, let's catch up."

"That would be great. Text my assistant and she'll set something up."

I hang up the phone glad I reached out to Tad. It never hurts to have a demigod in your back pocket.

My phone buzzes. It's a message from Scott. "In Mr. Bullock's office in five."

❧

STANDING YET AGAIN MR. BULLOCK'S OFFICE, looking out at the downtown Los Angeles skyline, I glance over at the empty walnut desk.

Scott comes in with Fiona and Renoir in tow. He gives me a smile. "You beat us to a meeting for once."

Fiona gives me a wink. "He wasn't in *The Pit* when he got the message."

Scott's eyes narrow. "Oh, really?"

"I took a bathroom break."

The baritone voice of Mr. Bullock fills the room. "Those are allowed Mr. Pennington. Did you tell them about the new moniker?"

Scott shakes his head. "No, sir."

Mr. Bullock beams. "Good." He motions for us to take the back leather parsons chairs that materialize in front of the walnut desk. Fiona must be bonding well with Renoir already as the poodle doesn't flinch at two large objects suddenly appearing in the room.

Fiona signals for Renoir to heel behind the chair on the left and then sits down. I grab the one on the right.

Mr. Bullock gives Fiona a smile. "It appears you have already made progress training Renoir."

"Yes, sir. She is so bright, it is a breeze."

He nods. "I'm glad you are discovering why poodles are known for their intelligence. But I didn't bring you here to chat about dogs. I wanted to inform you of a new case and a new moniker. As this is yet another possible murder case with an unusual weapon, I've decided team D & S should be called something far more appropriate. The Unusual Death Squad."

Fiona claps her hands together. "Oh, sir, it's brilliant. The moniker fits us to a T."

He glances at Scott who is hovering just behind us. "I must give credit to Mr. Pennington; he thought of it after the new case came in. The most unusual case yet."

Once again, as with my previous superior, Mr. Bullock really likes to keep his employees in suspense. "All right, sir. I'll bite. What is the new case?"

Mr. Bullock stands up from behind his desk and thrusts his hands out on the top of his desk as if he is going to perform a magic card trick. "Death by beer."

3

———

ZOOMER DRIVER REVISITED

Speeding away from my bungalow, I wish I could stay at home with Fiona instead of having to start my second job as a Zoomer driver. Yet, I can never say no to the Order, so I head out into the Los Angeles night as I had done for so many years. I head back onto the 405 freeway and my first ride buzzes through on my dash screen. A smile spreads across my face when I see the name.

"Hey Der, I was so excited to see your handle back on the Zoomer driver app. I've missed you so much. Pick me up in twenty minutes in front of the Matchbox."

What is Krissy doing at the Matchbox at seven at night? The famous dance club doesn't even open its doors until ten o'clock. I must admit I'm not surprised she is at the club of the moment. Krissy knows how to keep her name in the tabloids.

33

I get off at the La Brea off ramp and head toward central LA. According to a blast on my LA happenings feed, Matchbox has moved to a new location in an old warehouse in Koreatown and they've done a complete revamp of the club design. I punch the name into the GPS and my hunch is confirmed. The club is on Wilshire Boulevard right on the edge of Koreatown. I take a few of my hard-earned short cuts to avoid the traffic as people are still heading home from work. Even after jig zagging my way through side streets, I still get to the club a tiny bit late.

Krissy stands near the club entrance in a short gold-sequined mini skirt, a black crop top showing off her perfect flat stomach and a pair of killer knee-high black boots. Even though it's at least seventy degrees out, Krissy is shivering as she hovers near the curb. Boy, am I going to get an earful for making her wait.

I pull up in front of where she is standing and get ready to stop the car and open the door for her as I normally do. I never get the chance as she yanks open the door and plunges into the back seat like she's diving into a swimming pool. "Could you take any longer? Your Zoomer skills have slipped."

I smile at her in the rear-view mirror. "Good to see you too, Krissy. I should have guessed you'd be cranky. What is it, something like three days before the full moon?"

She kicks the back of my seat. "Yes. Which means you should be extra nice to me."

Werewolves are so high maintenance. "Sorry, I'll do

better next time. So why were you at the club? Isn't it a bit early for any action?"

She gives me one of her pouty smiles. The smile she gets paid big bucks for, and the one that has graced the cover or all the top fashion magazines.

"For a shoot, of course. They totally revamped the club in its new location and *Mademoiselle* wanted to use it for their September issue. I hear they are having a huge relaunch party next week."

With a devilish grin on my face, I say, "You know I'm just back in the country, how could I not know that?" She smacks the back of my seat as I pull away from the curb and back out onto Wilshire. "Because you're a damn wizard."

I love how we've been away from each other for months, yet we can slip right back into our friendship like a glove. "Where to now?"

She sighs. "To Café Charles on South La Brea. I have a dinner date with a new guy. I'm really not that into him despite how much he looks like an old rock and roll idol, but you know how it is before the full moon."

Werewolves and their insatiable sexual appetite which grows super charged before they transform. "Right. Hope he's at least a good lay," I say as I put the restaurant name into my GPS."

She sighs. "He's okay. But I've had better. Sometimes a girl has to lower her standards and take what is available." She leans over and seductively runs her bright red manicured nails down my arm. She purrs,

"How about you, Der? Are you available? I can ditch Rex in a second."

I must give Krissy credit for her persistence. She still hasn't given up her hot pursuit of me even after all this time. "Sorry, I'm seeing someone."

As Krissy leans back in the seat, her long blond hair falls over her shoulders like a curtain. She lets out a deep sigh. "It's that striking Indian partner of yours, isn't it? Anyone could see your chemistry together."

"Yes, it's Fiona. It took me flying all the way to London and solving another case with her for things to change in my favor. She is a consummate professional. Yet, I am happy to tell you she has finally succumbed to my charms."

Krissy laughs. "Wow, she sure played hard to get. But I hear Brit girls can be standoffish. Plus, they are experts at playing hard to get." She gives me a wicked smile. "Took all of ten minutes to win me over."

She always knows how to give me an ego boost. "Aw, shucks. Bet you say that to all the wizards you meet."

Krissy leans between the seats and blows a hot blast of air towards my ear. "Only the special ones."

Enough fun banter, I better get down to some Order business. Krissy is one of the biggest gossips around. "Any new paranormal gossip you can dish out? Did I miss anything good while I was gone in London?"

She sucks in a breath. "Oh, did you ever. There was a big showdown between a rival gang of vamps. A fellow werewolf was caught munching down on a deer in Griffith Park. And the hot couple of the moment is a demigod and a succubus. Everyone wants to be seen hanging out with them."

Interesting. The shifter disguised as a demigod has been busy. It seems he isn't shy about calling attention to himself. "They sound interesting. I'd love to meet them. Could you introduce me?"

"Of course," Krissy says with the confidence of a famous model soon to be budding starlet. "There's a big party at The Chateau Marmont Friday night. Get there around midnight and I'll introduce you. Bring your girl!"

I pull up in front of the Café Charles restaurant. The stately brick façade accented by bright white trim would be more at home in New Orleans than Los Angeles. A handsome man about six feet with broad shoulders and the retro looks of Elvis is hovering in front of the large, paneled wood door. "Is that Rex in the skintight navy-blue suit?"

She nods. "Yeah, he is nice to look at, and the whole young Elvis vibe he has is cool for sure. If only he was better in bed." She opens the door. "Guess you can't have everything."

I watch as she struts up to Rex and fawns all over him. Anyone looking at her would think she is madly in love. That she can't live without Rex. I can tell Rex is totally into her. As she snuggles close to him, and he leads her inside the restaurant, any doubts I had about Krissy's acting talents have vanished. There is an excellent chance her dream will come true, and she will make it as an A-list movie actress.

THE SOUND OF DOGS BARKING WAKES ME UP FROM A sound sleep. Holmes sits on one side of the sofa bed glowering at me. "You did something to the poodle didn't you?"

Renoir sits on the opposite side of the bed. In her wonderful sing-song French accented English she says, "I'm forever grateful to you, Mr. Dunne. Your dog tried to assault me this morning when I came out to procure some breakfast."

Good thing I had the foresight to cast a chastity belt protection spell last night. It seemed like a necessity knowing how Holmes can't stay away from poodles. I give Holmes the sternest father face I can muster this early in the morning. "Holmes, Renoir is not a poodle conjured to give you pleasure. She is a colleague, and you will treat her as such. Do you understand?"

He hangs his head, his long ears slightly covering his face. "I'm sorry. I was waking up out of a dream and saw a poodle and I just..."

I held my finger up to my lips. "That is all we are going to say about the subject. If we have another incident, I will have to take drastic measures." I look down at his nether regions. "Is that understood?"

A round of applause sounds from the hallway. Renoir uses her mistress's arrival to extradite herself from the situation. Fiona strokes Renoir's back. "You will make an impressive father one day, Mr. Dunne."

There is something so sexy about the way she says

my last name. I give her a sleepy smile. "Thank you, but I'd as soon not have to deal with children just yet."

Fiona chuckles and heads to the kitchen. "Seems you already have one, whether you like it or not."

Holmes puffs out his chest. "I am not a child. I am a full-grown canine."

We both ignore him. I pull the covers back and join Fiona in the kitchen. She eyes my bare chest. "I guess you run hot at night."

From any other woman, I'd take that as a come on but from Fiona it is a factual observation. "Yep. Even when it gets into the forties at night, I still can't wear a pajama top."

She eyes the inside of the refrigerator that is totally devoid of food. "I hate for you to have to conjure breakfast again."

I run my fingers through my rumpled hair. "It's not a problem. But as we are running a bit late, I'll conjure us up two protein shakes. Chocolate or vanilla?"

"I'll have chocolate. Can you add a few fresh raspberries for garnish?"

I give her a deep bow. "As you wish mistress."

She laughs. "Are you sure you were Zoomer driving last night? Sound like you might be moonlighting as a genie."

"You're a detective." I give her waist a squeeze. "You figure it out."

Fiona runs her hand down my chest. "Challenge accepted."

With a snap of my fingers, breakfast is served.

Because we are running late, I down mine in three gulps and Fiona takes hers into the bedroom so she can get dressed. I could get used to a routine like this, but Fiona is serious about getting her own place. And if I'm being practical, two large dogs and one more person makes my bungalow feel like a tiny house.

I snap my fingers again, and I'm dressed for work wearing black trousers and a gray button-down shirt. No need to wear a jacket as our first stop is the coroner's office. I'll bring my suit jacket to look official just in case we can squeeze in an interview with a witness.

Fiona strolls out wearing a navy-blue pants suit with a pale blue silk blouse. The contrast of colors makes her black hair shine even brighter. She taps her thigh and Renoir trots over. Fiona glares at Holmes who moves behind me as if I'm a shield. "You know the rules, Holmes. Be respectful of Renoir. Also please try to be a good example for her. She is new to the job as you once were."

Holmes nods but remains behind me. I must admit when Fiona turns on her strict teacher attitude, I'm a bit scared too. Yet, in the most cheerful voice I can muster, I say, "Okay gang, it's off to work we go."

Fiona moves next to me and puts a hand on my shoulder. "You look totally burnt out. "I'll drive us to the coroner's office."

I look over at Fiona, grateful that she offered to drive. After I dropped Krissy off at the restaurant last night, I had a series of calls for rides all over town. The last one was all the way out in the Valley. It was going to take some time for my Zoomer skills to return.

Opening the back door, I signal for Holmes to sit all the way over behind the driver's seat. Renoir dutifully sits behind the passenger seat. I point to both of them. "Let's have a nice, quite, uneventful trip, okay?"

Renoir nods and Holmes glares at me, then plants his nose against the window with total fascination as if there is a pterodactyl flying around the car.

Fiona starts up the engine and backs out of the driveway without using the camera. Her driving skill is impressive. She turns the wheel and heads down a series of side streets until she hits the freeway on ramp. "I can see why you love your car so much. It drives like a dream."

I stroke her hand that looks quite elegant wrapped around the leather steering wheel. "Now, don't get any ideas about..." It's funny but at that moment I realized in all the years I've had my Beemer I never gave her a name—it was time. "Greta."

Fiona chuckled. "You named your car Greta?" Fiona's nose crinkles. "Not exactly an appropriate name for such a sexy car."

"What do you mean? I'll have you know Greta is a sexy name in Germany. I know she is way before my time, but my great grandfather loved Greta Garbo, so I saw a few of her movies as a kid. She was super sexy in *Mata Hari*."

"Oh, I love *Mata Hari*. They made a Bollywood version which is hysterical."

I chuckle. "Whenever I'm down I love to watch an over-the-top Bollywood movie it never fails to cheer me up. No offense. I'm sure they do some wonderful art films in India."

Holmes, whose nose has not left the window the entire ride, finally chimes in. "I agree with you, Indian films can be amusing. One day I watched one called, *Idiots*. An unfortunate title for a humorous movie."

Fiona chuckles. "That is such a crazy film. The romantic fantasy scenes with the lead male and female's characters are my favorite part. The humor is a bit too slapstick for me."

"Oh, I liked the silly parts. Humans acting stupid are one of my favorite things," says Holmes a bit too gleefully.

Once again, I wonder when Holmes is sneaking in TV movie time, but it's my fault for leaving him alone so much. "I feel the same way about Bollywood romances and superhero films. They always put a smile on my face. What a wonderful thing to have in common."

The thought of a lazy Saturday evening curled up with Fiona watching a Bollywood classic sounds like Heaven.

Renoir decides to join in the conversation. "I have not had the pleasure of watching films from India. But if my mistress allows it, I would very much like to have the opportunity to see one."

Fiona signals to merge right as she works her way across two lanes of traffic. The examiners office is the next off ramp. She looks at Renoir in the rearview mirror. "Then let's pick a day this week to have an Indian movie night."

I sigh. "I wish I could join in the fun, but I have my Zoomer duties."

Fiona touches my hand resting on the console. "Sorry, I forgot your evenings are not your own."

"I wish I could. Hopefully I'll find the information the Order wants and then I will be free for the next Indian movie night." With Krissy's help, it might happen sooner than later.

Fiona crosses her fingers on the steering wheel. "Here's hoping you get a reprieve."

The Beemer speeds down the off ramp and onto the familiar block that houses the Wizard Medical Examiner's office. It is discreetly housed in a standard brick government building to fool outsiders. But inside the whole place is run by magic.

Fiona parks the car in the visitor spot, and I let the dogs out of the back. Clipping on their leashes, I slip into father mode once again. "I ask that you be on your best behavior, as animals are usually not allowed inside. Please listen closely so you both know all the details of the case. You are our backups after all. Is that understood?"

Holmes mumbles something under his breath while Renoir merely nods her elegantly groomed head as I hand her over to Fiona. Once inside, I remember about the overpowering smell of chemicals. They are going to drive both the dogs' crazy, but especially Holmes. I snap my fingers and cast a spell so the dogs' sense of smell is greatly reduced. I'd do the same for myself as the chemicals are gag worthy, but I need to learn that unpleasant smells come with being a detective for WI-6.

Fiona doesn't hesitate as she punches in the security code. Inside, she makes a beeline for the metal table where the medical examiner is. Thankfully he is standing in front of the only stainless-steel table with a body resting on it.

The examiner looks up and smiles. "Why, Ms. Singh. I wasn't expecting to see you again." He glances over at me. "And I'm surprised to see you back in Los Angeles, Mr. Dunne. I thought you would fall in love with London and never return to the States."

I laugh. "I have to admit it was tempting. London is a stunning city. The WI-6 headquarters is located in the iconic Gherkin building. Who wouldn't want to work there? But when Ms. Singh offered to return with me to Los Angeles, I knew I was taking the best part of London back with me."

Fiona beams while Holmes pretends to gag violently.

The medical examiner rushes to his side. "Is your canine all right Mr. Dunne? Does he need medical assistance?" He turns to me, concern flooding his face. "Didn't you cast a spell to protect him from the chemical odors?"

I walk over and pat Holmes on the back knowing his whole act was because I said something romantic about Fiona. "Yes, I cast the spell, but maybe I need to make it a bit stronger." I snap my fingers and cast a silence spell to muzzle Holmes. The last thing I need is for him to cause another scene.

The medical examiner walks back toward the body relieved. "This is Mr. Grump senior. He seems to have died from over consumption of beer according to the police report. His alcohol blood saturation was high enough to kill him at 1.40. Interesting enough he also had an elevated concentration of yeast in his blood which was high enough to cause candidemia."

Fiona sucks in a breath. "That type of an infection can causes organ failure and death."

The medical examiner's eyes brighten. "Yes, it can. But it is unusual for someone to have both alcohol intoxication and yeast concentrations at those amounts." He runs his fingers through his graying hair. "It is a perplexing case. What does your gut tell you, Mr. Dunne?"

My gut sits silent taking it all in. "Why did the police think Mr. Grump died from drinking too much beer?"

"The report says his home was littered with beer bottles and his trash can was full to the brim as well."

Fiona motions for the examiner to pull the covering off the body. Her eyes scanned the remains of Mr. Grump. "His pallor is a very strange color. Almost like jaundice."

The examiner nods. "That is not uncommon with candidemia."

I walk over to the examiner's computer. "Can I see the report? I'd like to know what Mr. Grump did for a living. If it was something stressful that would cause him to over drink."

The medical examiner's demeanor changes from serious to one of amusement. "He was part of a performing team, Grump and Son."

Fiona's brow furrows. "Team. Where they ..."

I cut in before she can complete her thought. "What did they do? Run a crew to hold beer bong parties at college fraternities?"

Despite the grim situation, the medical examiner chuckles. "Good guess, but no. Believe it or not, they were a magic act."

4

GRUMP AND SON

As we leave the examiner's office my heart feels heavy. This is another murder, I'm certain of it. Is this yet another life lost due to the handiwork of Mr. Pierre, or is it another killer intent on taking out wizards?

Fiona looks over at me as she clicks on the Beemer key and puts Renoir in the backseat. "Penny for your thoughts?"

"What do you think of the new case?" I ask as I put Holmes behind the driver's seat and climb into the passenger seat dreading her answer.

She starts up the engine then shuts it off again. "I think we are back where we started when we had the health nut case. This smacks of a killer with a vendetta against wizards posing as magicians. It could even be a jealous magician's handiwork."

I nod. "Yes, this time I don't think Mr. Pierre is involved. He must have something else up his sleeve."

Fiona cracks a smile. "I like your magician reference."

"Excuse me," says a French accented voice from the backseat. "May I make an observation?"

Fiona looks at Renoir in the rearview mirror. "Certainly."

She sits forward to be closer to her mistress. "I think there is only one cause of death, not two."

Holmes chimes in, "If my experience with the Los Angeles police department is any indication, their conclusion that Mr. Grump died of alcohol intoxication should be questioned."

"I agree," I say, wishing this conversation was back at the bungalow. "I think we should start as we always do with the prime witness and possible number one suspect, Mr. Grump's son. He is the one who was with his father when he died."

Fiona starts the car back up and pulls out her phone. "I'll do the honors. Maybe a female voice will get a better response."

"Go for it."

Fiona dials the number in the report, and it goes to voicemail. "This is Buddy Grump. I'm out purchasing a new wand. Please leave a message and I'll get back to you as soon as I can."

"It seems the son has a sense of humor. At least on his message."

Fiona guns the engine, frustrated. "Where to now?"

"May I suggest a quick walk before the day gets busy?"

Renoir barks in agreement. "It would be nice to stretch my legs, they are tres rigide."

Fiona pulls up the GPS map. "Let me see. In case we hear back from Mr. Grump, we should find a park near his house in Silver Lake." She runs her finger over the map. "I found the perfect spot. Silver Lake Meadows Park."

I pull out my phone and Google the park. Scrolling through the pictures I know it's the perfect choice. "Holmes you are going to love it. The park is next to a small reservoir that is known for its Mallard ducks."

He perks up in the back seat. "Brilliant. I can get some chasing in."

Renoir's nose twitches. "Chasing what?"

Her apprehension is understandable after this morning's episode with Holmes.

Holmes looks at her confused. "Why the ducks, of course."

She exhales hard. "Superb."

Fiona works her way through the city streets of Silver Lake and follows the signs for Silver Lake Meadow Park. This part of Los Angeles has a funky fun vibe, but I will be sure to cast a protection spell on my Beemer. It's ripe for car thieves.

Fiona finds a place to park down from the reservoir. She turns to face the dogs. "We will take a little walk around the lake. Please be on your best behavior." She eyes Holmes. "And absolutely no talking or muttering under your breath, is that understood?"

Holmes makes a snuffling noise. "You both are starting to sound like overbearing parents."

I reach over and tap his nose. "If you were more well behaved you wouldn't have to be lectured." I give Renoir a smile. "Not you, of course. You are a complete angel."

Renoir bobs her head and the black puff on top sways back and forth like ships at sea. "Thank you, monsieur."

While Fiona tends to Renoir, I grab Holmes's leash and clip it on his collar. He lumbers out of the backseat like a bear. With all the people milling about I enter his mind so I can speak with him. "Really, Holmes, you need to step up your game or Renoir is going to be the star detective dog."

He swings his big ears back and forth, not used to me entering his mind. Then he says, "There is no way possible to outshine her. Look at that elegant prance in her walk, she's stunning."

"I think her mistress is as well, but I don't find myself competing with her." I look down at Holmes. "Grow some balls or I'm going to think you are intimidated by a fluffy French poodle."

Holmes puffs out his chest and strides down the walkway to the lake. "You are right. I have to get over my infatuation with her."

I pat his rump. "There's the Holmes I know and love."

We soon catch up to Renoir and Fiona who are standing at the edge of the lake. Fiona gazes out at the body of water surrounded by a thick wall of concrete. "This is like no lake I have ever seen before. It looks like it is in prison with the large black fence around it and the thick concrete edge." Fiona shakes her head baffled by what she is seeing. "Why do they call this a lake?"

I chuckle. "It is actually an old reservoir that was used to store water for the area. That's why it looks so unnatural, because it is. Still, in the middle of the city people enjoy any type of water." I turn to Renoir whose gaze is fixed on the lake as well. "The fence is to keep animals and people out. Unfortunately, in the past several people have tried to kill themselves."

Fiona shakes her head. "That is horrible. Let's keep walking there is a large grassy area to the left."

Fiona stops walking when her phone buzzes in her purse. She pulls the phone out, checks the number, and smiles. Renoir heels at her side like a perfectly trained dog that has received hours of training. While Holmes tugs on his lead yanking me forward when he spies a duck waddling along the lake edge. I yank him back so I can hear Fiona's conversation.

"Hello, this is Ms. Singh speaking. I'm so sorry for your loss. My partner and I are private detectives working for a client who wants to stay anonymous. Yes, we would like to speak with you. Do you have any time today? We would greatly appreciate it. Oh, wonderful, see you in an hour."

It's so strange to listen to only one side of a conversation, but it is obvious Fiona's phone skills have come through yet again.

"Great job. It still amazes me how the witnesses never say no to you."

She smiles. "Trust me it has taken years of practice. You'll get the skill soon enough."

"How did Mr. Grump's son sound?"

"His name is Buddy, and he sounds pretty shaken up. He lost a father and a performance partner."

"Yes, he must be heartsick. But part of me feels sorry for him for another reason."

Fiona's brow furrows. "Why?"

"Because can you imagine how much he must have been teased in grade school with a name like Buddy Grump?"

"You have a point. We should be gentle with him for many reasons." Fiona eyes the meadow. "We should let the dogs frolic in the grass and then we can head off to meet Mr. Grump."

"Sounds good." Holmes tugs on his lead as he plows toward the meadow scattered with a few wildflowers. Three other smaller dogs are chasing each other off leash. I pop into Holmes's mind. "Don't get any ideas. I'm not going to let you run free."

"You don't trust me to behave myself?"

"No, I don't. You may not think that I am observant, but I saw the male Mallard duck wander over to the left side of the meadow and I knew right where you would head."

Holmes jerks his lead. "Balls. You would spoil my fun."

Fiona glances over and sees I'm not taking Holmes's leash off and does the same with Renoir. Though I doubt it is necessary. I'm sure Renoir will behave like the perfect lady canine she is.

We stroll around the meadow keeping a distance from the small dogs. The last thing we need is one of the ordinary dogs to sense something is wrong with ours. Unfortunately, my plan is foiled when the terrier comes racing toward Holmes.

His owner, a thin woman brunette wearing clothes that make it look like she just left a yoga studio, chases after him. "Charlie, get back here. I swear you'll never go off-leash again if you don't get back here right this minute."

Fiona chuckles. "You'd think Charlie was magical. She truly thinks he understands her."

As the little dog runs right up next to Holmes, I have my fingers at the ready. I pop into Holmes's mind. "Just sit still. I'll handle Charlie."

He glares up at me. "You better or I might have to stop him myself."

Hoping Charlie is as harmless as he looks, I reach down to try to pet him. "Hi, Charlie, this is Holmes. He's kind of shy so you better give him some space."

Charlie sniffs the air and sneezes. Do magical dogs have a smell normal dogs can't tolerate?

The thin brunette reaches down and grabs Charlie. "I'm so sorry. He's normally good with other dogs." She looks at Holmes and smiles. "But I don't think he's ever seen a bloodhound before. He's a curious dog."

"It's fine. He just gave him a good sniff, and that's it."

She laughs. "Oh good." She taps Charlie on his nose. "He does love to smell things. Hope you have a good day."

As I watch her stride out of the meadow, I wonder just how different Holmes smells. Then it hits me. Normal dogs stink when they get wet. Yet, Holmes doesn't smell at all. I must give Mr. Bullock credit. He created not only a hassle-free pet, but one devoid of the usually unpleasant dog smells. Well, except one—dog farts. I chuckle to myself, and Fiona comes striding over with Renoir. She's tucked a pretty pale pink wild-flower under the poodle's collar. "Looks like you handled that crisis well."

I glance down at Holmes. "Yes, we did. But it might not have gone so well. You trusted us enough to leave us alone?"

"I wasn't worried. I could always shift into a dog and rescue Holmes from the terrier."

"Right. I forgot about your special talent."

I wonder if Fiona's shifter dog would smell different as well.

She points to her smart watch. "I think we better leave soon. We certainly don't want to cause Mr. Grump any more stress by being late for his interview."

We walk at a brisk pace out of the park and down to the Beemer. I suck in a breath when I see someone has poured a soda all over the driver's side of the car. "Crap, they must have tried to break in and got ticked off and threw their soda at the car."

Fiona touches the sticky mess that left a stain on the window with one of her fingers, shakes her head, and then opens the back door for the dogs. "It would have been far worse if you hadn't done the protection spell."

I nod. "Right. I can't protect it fully as I don't want the thieves to get suspicious. They probably tried to key it too, but no way would the spell allow that. So, they used the drink as their only means of protest."

Fiona gets in and turns on the engine. "What am I going to do when I get a car?"

I give her a wink. "If it's magical, you have nothing to worry about."

Fiona strokes my hand seductively. "Is that a promise?"

"It is. When you get your new place, my present to you will be a magical car."

She kisses my cheek. "I'm starting to like dating a wizard."

I reach over and take her hand. "We do have our benefits."

As she pulls away from the curb, I hope I will one day show her the other benefits of dating a wizard. We don't have a reputation of being good lovers for nothing.

She follows Silver Lake Drive down to Lakewood Avenue and we are soon parking in front of 2426. It's an unassuming 1940s English cottage style stucco home that has a quaint arched wood door as it's only touch of character.

Fiona puts the car in park and takes in the home. "I guess magicians don't make very much money. The home can't be more than four hundred and fifty-seven meters."

Once again Fiona is fooled by a simple Los Angeles vintage home. "Actually, the house is probably worth a million and a half dollars."

She shakes her head in disbelief. "I know New York and San Francisco real-estate is overpriced as is London's, but I had no idea Los Angeles's was as well."

Holmes cranes his neck so he can see past the fluffy fur ball on Renoir's head. "I agree with Fiona's astonishment. There is nothing noteworthy about the homes exterior except the arched door and the triangular shaped chimney."

"Welcome to Los Angeles's crazy inflated real estate market," I say as I open my passenger door.

Fiona stays put. She mutters something to the dogs and then opens and closes her door. "I think it's best we leave the dogs out of this interview. I promised them a treat after we are done."

"I agree. Do you want to lead the questioning or are we going to play it by ear?"

She walks up the pathway that leads to a set of stairs. "As the house is set into a hill, we need to take the steps to get to the front door." Fiona squeezes my hand before she rings the doorbell. "This case is a difficult one. Don't be afraid to ask the tough questions."

The sound of heavy footsteps grows closer and then the door opens to reveal a tall thin man with medium brown hair and a pair of horn rimmed glasses. He looks as if he hasn't slept in several days.

Fiona sees that he is struggling, so she holds out her hand. "I'm Ms. Singh and this is my partner Mr. Dunne. Is it all right if we come in, Mr. Grump?"

He blinks hard then nods. "Sorry, I'm a bit sleep deprived. Come in."

We enter the living room that has a wood beamed ceiling and a triangle shaped fireplace that mimics the chimney, which is quite striking and unexpected in a vintage home.

Mr. Grump follows my gaze. "The unusual fireplace is the reason I bought the place."

He motions to a leather sofa facing the hearth. "Have a seat." Then he moves to a club chair loaded down with photo albums and sets them on the hardwood floor. "I've been looking through photographs for my father's memory board."

My mouth goes dry, thinking I will face the same thing when both my parents die. Even though we aren't close now due to my career choice, they gave me a wonderful childhood.

Fiona, sensing the mood in the room, reaches over and takes one of the photo albums and starts to thumb through it. "It seems your father was a magician for most of his life. When did you become part of his act?"

He sinks back in his chair. "I think I must have been ten when he first asked me to join him on stage. My whole body shook. I was so scared." He rubs his hands together reliving the memory. "But by the third time, I started enjoying helping him with his acts. My mother didn't approve. She thought it would rob me of a normal childhood, so I didn't grace the stage again until after she left my dad."

Buddy Grump seems like a simple unassuming man, but like many people there is a story of pain and loss behind his eyes.

"That must have been a difficult life for you to grow up in."

He let out a sigh. "It had its moments. But everything became wonderful when we were up on stage. My father taught me all of his tricks. I understood why he neglected my mother and me once I began performing. The joy you can bring to people's lives through magic is truly intoxicating. Yet, a blessing and a curse."

If only Buddy knew what real magic could do. When the medical examiner told me the Grumps' profession, for a second I wondered if they were fellow wizards moonlighting as magicians. But my gut told me no. Once again it turned out to be right.

Fiona holds open the album to a picture of Grump Senior holding a water bottle upside down while putting a nail inside, yet no water seemed to have dripped out. "This trick must have been popular. It looks truly astonishing."

Buddy beams. "It is one of two tricks my father was

famous for. The miracle bottle always was a showstopper." He leans forward in his chair. "Would you like to see it?"

Fiona's eyes light up. "Oh, I would love to. But please, don't feel you need to indulge me."

Buddy rubs his hands together and stands up. "I think it would be good for me to do some magic. Since Father passed away, I have had no desire to do tricks—until now."

He pops down the hallway and we hear some rummaging noises and then he returns with a Coke bottle and an empty water pitcher. He puts the bottle on the end table near the club chair and then vanishes behind a small door near the entryway and returns with the pitcher that is now full of water. He pulls a few nails out of his pocket and motions for Fiona to stand next to him. "Please fill the bottle to the brim."

Fiona's hands shake and she spills a bit of water out of the pitcher as she moves it next to the bottle. "I'm so sorry. But I've never been part of a magic trick before."

Buddy smiles. "There is a first time for everything."

I chuckle as Fiona lifts the pitcher and fills the bottle to the brim slowly so as not to spill any more water. "Now what do I do?"

"Put the pitcher on the end table and then sit down and enjoy the show."

Fiona claps her hands like a little kid. "Oh, I can't wait!"

She sits down next to me and, forgetting herself for

a moment squeezes my hand. Luckily Buddy doesn't notice. He's too busy slowly turning the bottle upside down.

Fiona applauds. "Marvelous! There isn't even one drop of water on the floor."

Buddy waves his hand underneath the bottle, then picks up two nails with his other hand. Fiona's eyes grow wide as he pushes the nail into the bottle and only one drop of water falls to the floor. He repeats the move with the second nail.

Fiona flies to her feet, applauding like an out-of-control fan. Buddy beams as he watches her childlike wonder. I know exactly how the trick is done and how the bottle has been modified, but I too stand and give Buddy a round of applause. "Wonderful trick." I give him a well-earned look of appreciation for his magic. "Amazing. And we are so close to you, and I still have no idea how you did it."

He gives us a quick bow and he flips the bottle over and puts it on the nightstand. "Thank you so much. It felt good to do the trick again. But you are not here for magic tricks."

No, we aren't, but it was a wonderful way to get him to relax.

Fiona sits back down and gets right back to business. "We only have a few questions for you, Mr. Grump."

He nods. "Go ahead."

"I understand you were performing when your father collapsed, is that the right?"

His face drains of color. "Yes, it was during our finale. Father was a consummate professional. He drank like a fish to try and forget my mother's desertion and unfortunately, he hasn't stopped for ten years. But he never missed a show. Somehow he always kept it together so he could support us."

I lean forward. "That is commendable. Can I ask if anyone else came to the stage?"

"Yes. She was a regular who came to our performances quite often. The woman always sat in the middle of the first row. A striking brunette with quite the figure. She was always impeccably dressed. The woman came backstage one time and I'll never forget how beautiful and charming she was. She tried to comfort me as I held Father in my arms."

This woman sounds promising. "That's wonderful. Did you happen to get her name?"

His brow furrows as his mind fights to stay in the present. "Yes." He closes his eyes and sits deep in thought for a moment. Then Buddy opens his eyes and stares right at me. "Her name is Rene Pearson."

5

GRUMP NO MORE

As soon as we are standing in front of Buddy Grump's home, Fiona pins me next to the car. "Who is Rene Pearson? Your face went as white as a ghost when you recognized her name."

"Let's get in the car and I'll explain it. Holmes and Renoir should know what we are dealing with."

"You're scaring me," Fiona says as she clicks the car doors open and we take our seats.

Holmes nudges my shoulder sensing something is up. "Something big happened inside, didn't it?"

Fiona doesn't start the engine, instead she turns toward me in her seat. "I thought witnessing an amazing magic trick up close was a big deal until the huge reveal at the end." She glowers at me. "A reveal only Derrick seems to know the meaning of."

Holmes nudges my arm. "Pray tell."

I sit back in my seat trying to figure out a short way

to fill them in on the most notorious succubus in LA history. "The woman who helped Buddy Gump when his father was dying is someone I know by reputation only. I'm at a loss as to why she attached herself to the Grumps, but I'm sure we can find out. Mrs. Pearson is a succubus."

Holmes growls while Fiona lets out a gasp. "They are real?"

"Oh, yes. Very. She has claimed her fair share of male victims. Tad Ryan knows everything about her. I'm going to need to set up a meeting with him. It seems my case for the Order and our new case for the WI-6 have one person in common. The succubus could be the key to solving both mysteries."

Fiona starts up the engine. "Should we try to fit in another witness while we wait? One of the men that knew Buddy Senior at his favorite bar?"

I pull out my phone. "No. I need to meet up with Ryan before my Zoomer duty." I text Tad's private number. "*911. Need to see you ASAP.*"

Fiona turns onto Lakewood and heads toward the freeway. "You aren't going to let me come along, are you?"

"No. I'm sorry. Why? Do you have the hots for Tad Ryan?"

She gives me a wicked smile. "What's not to love? Ripped abs, blond hair, and ocean blue eyes. He took my breath away in *Sun in Peru*."

I laugh, knowing there is no such movie. And if Fiona's interest in me is any indication, she is not into famous, blond, A-list actors. "You never know. I might be able to introduce you to him. Of course, the cases come first."

Holmes makes a harrumphing noise. "Really. The banter between you two is so boring. Tell me more about the succubus. Do they truly suck the life out of men?"

The thought gives me a chill. "Yes, they do. Rene Pearson is likely to be hundreds of years old, but she doesn't look a day over thirty-five."

Renoir shifts in the back seat. "In France a woman that old is off the shelf, as they like to say."

"Yes, Hollywood is the same. That's why her marriage to a top producer collapsed last year when he ran off with a twenty-two-year-old."

Renoir looks surprised. "Why didn't she kill her husband for such a betrayal?"

"It would seem quite suspicious for a top Hollywood producer to drop dead for no apparent reason," Fiona says, knowing how detectives would automatically think Rene killed her husband.

Renoir nods. "You have a point."

Fiona heads over to the 405 freeway. "We'll head home then."

My phone buzzes in my lap—it's Tad. *"911 sounds serious. I'm crazy busy doing a script run through but I have some time at 7:00 PM. Meet me at Smith's on Rodeo. Can you give me a heads up on what caused the 911 emergency?"*

"Rene Pearson."

"Crap."

I feel a bit guilty taking my name off the Zoomer app for a few hours but my meeting with Tad is that important. Hopefully Mr. Kumar will agree with me as I'm certain the Order wizards who monitor the app will see what I have done.

I make it to Beverly Hills in record time using a few of my tried and true shortcuts. I toss my key to the valet and head up the stairs to the Smith's entrance. The huge double doors are flanked by two large water features that bubble away creating a Zen-like experience before you enter the steakhouse.

An attractive brunette wearing the perfect little black dress greets me with a smile behind the hostess stand. "Do you have a reservation?" I totally forgot to make one but I'm certain Tad had his assistant make a reservation. But under what name? Tad was notorious for using fake names when he went out. "I'm here to meet someone."

She looks down at her reservation list. "Very good. What is the name?"

It sounds like such a simple question but not when you are dealing with an A-list celebrity that likes to keep the paparazzo at bay. My phone buzzes and I see it is text from Tad's number. *I'm in the back booth under the name of Gunderson. I'm wearing a large hat.*

Of course he is. I smile up at the hostess. "The name is Gunderson."

She runs her finger over the list and nods. "Yes. He's

at table twenty," she picks up the black leather-bound menu, "Follow me."

She leads me through a brightly lit main dining area filled with elegant tables surrounded by beautiful people. Then we get to an area at the back of the restaurant that can only be described as cave-like. Sitting in the left-hand corner booth is a man with a black Stetson hat. It's pulled way down over the man's eyes, but I would recognize that kilowatt celebrity smile anywhere—Tad.

I slide over on the other side of the booth, and he tips his hat up ever so slightly. "Good to see you, Derrick. It's been a while."

"It has. What's with the ridiculously huge Stetson hat?"

He sighs. "*The Star* wrote an article about how I've had work done. Like a demigod needs to get plastic surgery."

I laugh. "Right. But doesn't the hat make you look like you are hiding something?"

He beams. "I love to antagonize them. I'll keep it up for a few days and then show my face all over town. I'll make sure I show a hint of aging, so they don't get suspicious. Look at how the tabloids say Paul Rudd never ages and joke he is a vampire. But you aren't here to talk about my tabloid woes, are you?"

The waiter pops over to our table. "Would you gentlemen like a cocktail?" He points to the small menu in the middle of the table. "We have our specialty cocktail of course, but may I recommend the fizz martini? It's our bartender's latest creation."

Tad runs his finger down the drink menu and says, "I think I'll go classic tonight. I'll have a martini straight up."

The waiter turns to me. "And you, sir?"

I want a cocktail the size of Rhode Island, but I still must work. "I'll have a Perrier with lemon."

The waiter walks away, and Tad kicks me under the table. "Loosen up."

"Sorry, I have to work tonight. I'm back Zoomer driving remember?"

"Right. In that case let's get down to business. As you know Rene is a succubus. She is also a paranormal for hire. The demis use her once and while. But she isn't working for us now."

I lean back in the leather booth relieved. "Well, she happened to be at the scene of what I believe to be a murder. She is the number one witness."

Tad temples his hands together. "That is strange. Usually, she is quite discreet. Well, unless she is hunting a man."

It was hard to imagine her wanting either of the Grumps. Yet, there must be some kind of connection besides the possibility she is a magic fan. "I've met the son of the man that died. Neither of them are powerful men. Just good magicians."

"Ah, that must be her angle. Are you sure they aren't wizards? I hear you guys moonlight as magicians sometimes so you can practice your magic in plain sight. Guess it gives you guys a kick."

I chuckle. "Some lesser wizards. But no, they aren't wizards or anything paranormal that I can tell."

Our drinks arrive and Tad downs half of his. "There is only one way to know what she was up to that night —ask her."

"Can you introduce me? I've never met a succubus thankfully, but I heard they are suspicious of people they don't know."

"That is all too true. I'll have to set it up."

"Can my partner be there?"

Tad polishes off his drink. "Isn't your partner a woman? A beautiful one I hear."

"Yes. Why is that a problem?"

Tad waves the waiter away after he picks up his empty drink. "Rene will be threatened, of course. All male attention must be on her. I'll try to set up a meeting tomorrow. Just an FYI. You might need to cast a spell to protect yourself. She's a powerful seductress when she wants to be."

"Fine, but Fiona won't like me interviewing her alone."

Tad gives me one of his celebrity smiles. "That's your problem, not mine."

THE SOUND OF THE FRIDGE OPENING AND CLOSING wakes me up from a deep sleep. Fiona sits at the dining room table, sipping a glass of orange juice and eating a yogurt. Good thing I thought to conjure some food before I went to bed. Despite the fact the sofa bed is only a few feet away from her, Fiona scrolls through her laptop, unaware I'm awake. Renoir sleeps next to her feet in a pretty teal colored doggie bed Fiona must have purchased for her. She gives me a smile when she sees me sit up in bed. "Must have been a busy night Zoomer driving. I tried to wait up for you to tell you my news, but I couldn't keep my eyes open, so I went to bed."

I have some big news myself, but I'll let her fill me in first. Grateful I remembered to conjure my pajama bottoms, I get out of bed and sit across from her. "Tell me your big news."

"I found a flat. A wonderful place just two blocks from here with a view of the ocean and a small balcony where I can sit and enjoy the sound of the sea. It's quite small, but nothing like the tiny flats I've lived in back in London. I'll move my few things tonight after work."

Despite the fact I knew this day would come, I'm still a bit sad I'm losing my roommate. Forcing myself to sound cheerful, I say, "Oh, that's great. I hope I can visit you and we can listen to the ocean on the balcony together."

She reaches across the table and squeezes my hand. "Of course. I hope you will visit often."

Does that mean she wants our relationship to take the next step? Moving out makes sense, as we truly are on top of each other, yet the closeness has been nice. I give her hand a squeeze back. "You can count on it. As soon as my Zoomer job is done and I have my nights free again."

She closes her laptop and gives me her full attention. "What is your big news?"

The entire time I did my Zoomer pickups and drop offs last night, I ran through the perfect way to tell her about Rene Pearson. But as I look into Fiona's dark eyes, I draw a complete blank.

"You seem to be tongue tied. It seems it is not good news."

I run my fingers through my thick dark hair. "No, it isn't. I met with Tad last night and he filled me in about Mrs. Pearson."

Fiona gives me a weak smile. "That's not bad news. The more information we have, the easier it will be when we interview her."

I suck in a breath. "That's the thing. Tad told me it would be better if I did the interview alone."

Fiona pushes back her chair and stands up so quickly she almost trips over Renoir. "She's a succubus. You can't be alone with her. Who knows what she will do?"

In all my scenarios of Fiona's reaction I never imagined one this dramatic. I try not to smile knowing part of her reaction is because she is jealous. "It will be fine. I'll have the Order cast a powerful protection spell. She won't be able to sway me."

Fiona sits back down in defeat. "You have thought everything through, haven't you?"

"Yes, I had a lot of time to think between rides last night."

She stands back up and takes the empty glass and yogurt container to my tiny kitchen. "We better get ready. I lined up an interview with the manager of the club where Mr. Gump died. He is a key witness."

Despite being upset, Fiona shifts right into professional mode. "Oh, that's terrific. Thanks for setting that up."

She doesn't turn to face me. "It's my job."

DRIVING TOWARD THE CLUB SANS THE DOG'S, I expected Fiona to give me the cold shoulder. Instead, she insists we stop at McDonald's drive through. Without asking me what I want for breakfast, she buys me an egg Mc Muffin. Fiona knows me well. She gives me a satisfied smile as I bite off a huge mouthful and a chunk of egg sticks to my chin.

She laughs. "I think you call it dashboard dining. Truly disgusting."

I take a napkin out of the bag and wipe off my mouth. "Hey, a guy has to do what a guy has to do."

She doesn't laugh, instead she turns left down Wilshire Boulevard. "The magic club is in an old theater called the Rialto."

"Oh, I think I saw an article about the conversion to a club. The pictures were stunning. I can't wait to see what it looks like in person."

She gives me a smile like one a mother would give her child when they said something silly. "Remember we are there for work, not fun."

I polish off my McMuffin and toss the wrapper in the bag. Good thing Holmes wasn't with us, or he would have been begging for a piece of my egg sandwich. As we get closer to the address the front of the Rialto comes into view. The peacock-colored art deco trim that surrounds the marquee is a sad reminder of why we are here. In bold black letters still on the marque are the words: **Grump and Son Tonight**!

Fiona pulls her eyes off a parking spot and follows my gaze. "Oh, that is so sad. I bet they haven't had the heart to remove it."

"You are probably right. It's been almost two weeks since Mr. Grump died."

Fiona deftly parks the Beemer as if she has been driving it for far longer than two days. "How do you want to do the interview with the theater manager, Mr. Mayflower? Tag team him or see whom he responds to the best?"

I grab the McDonald's bag not wanting to leave it in the car. "I think the last option is best."

Fiona clicks the key after we both exit the car. "Excellent choice."

We pause in front of the marquee, and I instinctively put my hand over my heart. "How sad. I doubt Buddy will ever be able to perform here again."

Fiona nods. "I know I certainly couldn't."

After paying tribute to Mr. Grump senior, we pull

open the heavy theater doors and enter a lobby fit for a queen. Huge, fluted gold columns frame either side of the theater entrance doors. The gilded plaster ceiling has various classic Greek gods and goddesses in the center of the medallions. A pair of impressive torpedo-shaped glass chandeliers hang down from the ceiling like giant icicles.

Fiona stands in the center of the red and gold floral designed carpet taking it all in. "This must have been a showstopper in its day. I can't wait to see what the theater looks like."

I wave my hand before me, signaling for her to follow me as I open the main door with a flourish and the scent of lilies drifts past my nose. Two huge floral displays frame the entrance.

Fiona sucks in a breath and stands frozen in place. "The restoration is award winning."

The amount of money that must have been spent to restore all the plasterwork and the gold gilding had to be in the millions. Normally this much gold and red would be beyond garish, but somehow the massive red velvet draperies that frame the private boxes covered in gold cording and tassels make for a delight for the eye.

A slightly chubby bald man wearing a nicely tailored suit strides into my peripheral view. "It is stunning, isn't it? Every day I pinch myself that I can work in such a magical place."

Enjoying the irony of his words, I hold out my hand. "I'm agent Dunne and this is agent Singh. We appreciate you setting aside a bit of time for us."

He points to the row of red velvet upholstered theater chairs next to us. "Have a seat. I have a meeting in twenty minutes with a magic team to replace the Grumps." He pushes out his lower lip as if he is fighting back tears. "I feel like a traitor, but the show must go on. Buddy has assured me he is done with performing for the immediate future. I would have been happy to have him as a single act, but I understand it isn't possible for him right now."

I take an instant liking to Mr. Mayflower. His compassion for Buddy shows he's not the typical hardened theater manager I thought he might be.

Fiona pulls out her phone. "Do you mind if we record this interview?"

Interesting, it must be some kind of test. She knows I can take notes in my head with my notation spell. Mr. Mayflower shows no signs of being nervous about being recorded at all. "No. I want to find out what happened as much as you do. Max was in excellent health for an eighty-year-old despite his love of cocktails. He held his liquor well and had the stamina of a forty-year-old, hard earned from all his years of doing vanishing acts and cutting women in half."

So, he thought something was off about Mr. Grump's death as well. "You never saw any signs of him struggling to do a trick or when he was using the stairs?"

As if I insulted him personally, Mayflower huffed out, "Of course not. I told you he was healthy. Far healthier than my own father."

Now the edge in his voice made sense. Watching Mr. Grump die in front of him made Mayflower think about how much time his father has left.

Fiona gently touches Mr. Mayflower's hand resting on the metal arm of the seat. "I'm sure he would appreciate how much you cared."

Mayflower looks up at Fiona. "I hope so. I cared about them both. They have been my headliners for almost a year."

Sensing we aren't going to get much more information from him I decide to ask him one last question. "Buddy told me there was a beautiful woman that was a regular at their shows. Did you ever speak with her?"

Mayflower's face crinkled up like he just sucked on a lemon. "There is something terribly wrong about her obsession with Buddy. She has a certain energy that makes me nervous when I'm near her."

I wish I could tell him his instincts are spot on. He should fear her. "So, you didn't like her."

He sat up in his seat. "No, I didn't. And if you ask me, she has something to do with Max's death."

6

THE SUCCUBUS DEFENSE

Fiona and I sit in the Beemer, still reeling from Mr. Mayflower's words. I turn to my beautiful partner who sits running her hands over the steering wheel as if she could wring the truth out of Mrs. Pearson. "Are you sure you don't want me to come as backup? I really don't feel comfortable letting you go alone."

After Mr. Mayflower's words, I have to admit my nerves were on edge as well. "I told you about the problem with bringing you along. Rene can't stand female competition."

Fiona continues to run her hands along the steering wheel until she stops abruptly. A wicked grin spreads across her face. "What if I come along but not as a woman?"

I wanted to smack my forehead for not thinking of it myself. "Of course. I keep forgetting you're a shifter."

She chuckles. "Well, it's not like I'm shifting around you all the time."

Her words make me wonder if she shifts more than I think. If I had the skill, I'd be testing out new forms all the time, just like Jennifer. That's why Brooklyn pegged her the girl chameleon.

Fiona snaps her fingers as if she was going to conjure something. "I know the perfect disguise."

"What? Are you going to shift into a mouse or something?"

She beams. "Something far better. I'm going to come as Holmes."

It's my turn to laugh. "I know someone who is going to have something to say about that."

The devilish grin returns to her face. "Holmes doesn't have to know."

Good thing he can't read minds, or her plan would be screwed. "It's an excellent idea."

"Now I just need Tad to set up a meeting with Rene and we can surprise her. I guess he's been too busy with his new film to follow up on his promise to set up the meeting."

Fiona's brow furrows. "I don't think that is the right approach. Once we show up, she'll just bolt."

"You have a point. Then we'll play it like we would any other witness, except I'll get her private line from Tad. Otherwise, she could evade us for days."

The sound of the engine purring to life is my signal to text Tad. "*Hey, mister sexiest man alive three times running, I know you're busy, but can you send me Rene's direct number pronto? Our key witness says he thinks Rene might have been involved in the murder of Mr. Grump somehow. Thanks."*

I turn to Fiona as she follows the GPS back to my bungalow in Santa Monica. "I need to move my stuff today. Maybe we can get it done before we hear from Mrs. Pearson."

My heart sinks a bit. Part of me had conveniently forgot she found a place. "I'm sure we have time. First, we have to hear back from Tad, then Rene. Both are Hollywood types. They aren't known for getting back to people quickly."

She chuckles. "For once I'm glad they are. Waiting always drives me bonkers."

I chuckle. "I've noticed."

We have a pleasant drive to my house. I occasionally point out landmarks, while Fiona tells me a bit more about her family. My hope is that she wants me to know them better as she sees a real future with me. Not that she is just filling time on the drive to Santa Monica.

She parks the car in the driveway. We get out and as we approach the front door, two distinct barks fill the air. One I'm very familiar with. The low, deep, guttural bark of Holmes. The other is a delicate, almost song-like bark from Renoir.

We open the door to much fanfare from the dogs. Renoir dances around Fiona and Holmes proceeds to slobber all over my shoes and trousers. I pat him on the head. "Can you please stop? I took a shower this morning."

Fiona kneels down and lets Renoir cover her in doggie kisses. "I missed you too. After our dinner, I'll take you for a walk at the new flat. There is a nice grassy area the put in just for dogs."

Renoir gives her a doggie smile. "Oh, I would so like that."

Once again, my heart sinks. My brain doesn't want to remember that Fiona is moving out today. I snap my fingers and a huge hamburger appears at Holmes's feet. "I hope this makes up for leaving you behind."

He harrumphs. "Hardly." Holmes tries to pretend he's not interested in the hamburger, but I notice the drool dripping out of the corners of his mouth. "Go ahead and eat. Stop torturing yourself."

Holmes dives for the hamburger and in less than a minute it is gone. I looked over at Renoir. "I'd be happy to conjure a treat for you too."

She looked up at me with her dark eyes with curiosity. "I can have whatever I desire?"

"Yes, anything."

"It would be a treat to have some steak tartare."

What a classically French thing for her to ask for. I snap my fingers and a perfectly plated steak tartare sits before her. Unlike Holmes, she takes tiny bites and savored each one.

When Renoir finishes her tartare, she has a look of sheer bliss on her face. "Magnifique." She looks over at her mistress. "Please don't take offense, but I will miss not living with a wizard."

Fiona gives me a smile. "It seems your charms work on female canines as well."

I chuckle. "Let's get you packed up and settled into the new place. Do you need me to conjure any furniture?"

Fiona shakes her head. "No, I went to West Elm and picked out everything. They delivered the living room furniture this morning."

I feel a bit hurt she didn't ask me to conjure her dream furnishings. "What about bedding?"

Fiona smiles. "That I have not had time to purchase."

I rub my hands together eagerly. "I'll get you outfitted in no time."

"You are going to spoil me."

I reach over and give her a hug. "It is my pleasure."

Fiona whispers in my ear, "Are you still going to conjure me a car as well?"

"A promise is a promise."

STANDING IN FIONA'S NEW FLAT, THE DÉCOR IS QUITE the contrast to my Craftsman bungalow. The walls are various shades of white from bright to one with a slight blue hue. It's an appropriate color living so close to the ocean. The large sliding doors in the living room frame a killer view of the beach with the ocean off in the distance. The living room furniture is also white. A small sectional, glass coffee table with white metal legs and a TV console made of raw wood give the room a tiny break from all the white. The only other color is from the black 65" TV.

Fiona points to a hall just past the small kitchen, again all white. The only relief from the monochrome color scheme is the silver color of the stainless appliance and the brushed brass hardware on the cabinets and the sputnik lighting.

I smile as I see Renoir trot over to her pristine white doggie bed. At least she adds some contrast to the living room with her black fur.

Fiona looks down at the bags and luggage we brought over from my place. "Would you mind taking my bags in the bedroom?"

I give her a mischievous smile. "Oh, so the first place you want me is in the bedroom?"

She gives my butt a slight tap. "Don't get excited. My bed hasn't arrived yet. I'll be sleeping on the couch tonight."

"Are you sure? You can use my bedroom one more night. I don't mind."

Fiona moves past me toward the bedroom. "No. The bed is being delivered first thing in the morning." She reaches over and strokes my cheek, her Shalimar perfume lingering under my nose. "You're sweet to think of me."

Like I can think of anything else these days. "We wizards aim to please."

Fiona gives me a wink. "I hope you mean that because I heard that wizards have large staffs."

A running joke in the paranormal world that happens to be true. Too bad I must leave for Zoomer duty soon. Fiona seems to be in a romantic mood. "Anything else I can do for you before I leave?"

She points to the kitchen counter. "Can you put the extra paper towels I bought up on the top shelf of the pantry?"

I smile. Fiona is five ten and can reach most of the cabinetry herself, but the top of the pantry is going to be a bit of a struggle for her. Not for me at over six feet. "Sure."

I grab two of the paper towel rolls and practically stand up on tiptoes to get them to stand up on the shelf. "Guess you don't think you need these for a while."

She chuckles. "I'm sure I'll find a way to get them down when I need them."

Once again, I have forget she is a shifter. She could shift into a giraffe to retrieve the towels if she wanted.

Fiona takes my hand in hers and walks over to the sliding door. A pleasant tingling sensation radiates through my hand as she opens the sliding door for me. "I want you to see the reason I rented this place."

The sound of waves crashing only steps from the condo and the distinct smell of the sea air fills my lungs. The balcony barely holds two small wicker chairs and a tiny table but there is no doubt it will be a haven for Fiona after a long day of detective work. A tinge of jealousy hits me. Being this close to the ocean was always a dream of mine but the best I could do without using magic is my little bungalow four blocks from the beach. "I admit I'm a bit jealous."

She leans over and lightly kisses my lips. "You can join me any time you wish."

If she keeps pouring on the charm, I will not want to leave for my Zoomer duty. With every ounce of willpower I can muster, I don't dive into her lips for more. My alarm on my smart watch thankfully goes off, reminding me it's time to start my first Zoomer shift. I pull her close to me and kiss her properly. A nice, long kiss. Then I break free, and she realizes I have to go. I touch the tip of her long, elegant nose. "I am going to hold you to the offer. As soon as the bed arrives."

DRIVING DOWN LA BREA ON THE WAY TO PICK UP Krissy from a photo shoot, my screen buzzes letting me know a text is coming in. *"Here's Rene's direct number, 232-444-666. But you're not going to need it. She invited me for a cocktail at the Polo Lounge at 11:30. I accepted the offer, but you will be the one who is going to meet her."*

The little hairs on the back of my neck stand to attention. At first, I wasn't going to take Fiona up on her offer to shift into Holmes for my meeting with Rene, but I will now. I can't imagine she will be pleased when I show up instead of Tad. I text back. *"I don't know how I'm ever going to repay you."*

Tad texts in all caps with a smiley face. *"DON'T WORRY I'LL THINK OF SOMETHING."*

Fantastic. Not only am I worried about the meeting with Rene, now I'm worried about what Tad's big payback request is going to be. He's a demigod so it's going to be epic, I'm sure. Still, it will be worth it if it helps the Unusual Death Squad solve another case.

But first I need to make two calls. The first to Krissy. She is not going to be happy when I break the news I can't pick her up. I bring my phone up on the screen and auto dial Krissy's number. She picks up on the first ring. "Hey Der, I'm running a bit late. The photographer is a real dickwad. Can you pick me up in an hour?"

Great, she's in a terrible mood. "Um. Something has come up. I must pull myself off duty tonight. I'm sure Brian will be happy to pick you up."

Mumbling comes through the car speakers. "I'm starting to really not like your partner. She is keeping me from my Derrick fix."

I chuckle. "Actually, it's not her fault. It's the Order."

She sighs. "They are way too demanding. I hoped your switching jobs would give you more time, but it seems you have double duty. At this rate, I'll never see you."

I can always count on Krissy for an ego boost. "I'll see you soon. The job for the Order is a quick one. Besides, aren't we going to meet at the party at the Chateau?"

I hear a slap. "Duh. I totally forgot." Her voice sounds brighter. "I'll see you tomorrow night then."

"Can't wait." Successfully having smoothed Krissy over, I don't think I will have as much luck with Fiona. Punching in her number, I cross my fingers she picks up.

She answers on the third ring. "Derrick, what a pleasant surprise. How is the Zoomer driving going?"

"I've had to take my name off the list for tonight."

"Oh, oh. That doesn't sound good."

"No. It's good news. Tad set up a meeting with Rene at 11:30 at the Polo Lounge. I want to take you up on your offer to help be my backup."

There is an excited tone in her voice. "Oh, how fun. I've heard about the famous Polo Lounge. Plus, I love shifting into animals. Becoming Holmes should be a treat."

I bite my lip and pull the car over, not willing to risk driving when Fiona hears my big request. Once I shut off the car, I continue. "Um, it's about turning into Holmes... I need you to shift into something else."

Fiona sounds a bit puzzled. "Not a problem at all. I'll shift into anything you want."

I swallow hard again. "I need you to shift into Tad Ryan."

THE LAST TIME I WENT TO THE POLO LOUNGE WAS with Tad. He wanted me to do him a favor and my reward was brunch at the lounge. This time I literally was sitting it out. Instead, I sit in my Beemer parked in the underground parking across the street from The Beverly Hills Hotel. My viewing screen lights up when Fiona, in the guise of Tad Ryan, drives past the iconic green and white hotel sign and past the tall palm trees that line the entrance to the hotel. She's driving Tad's gleaming red Lamborghini thanks to my magic. I enter Fiona's mind. "You are having way too much fun driving Tad's car."

Her beaming smile is visible in the rearview mirror. "I was thinking about how you promised to conjure me a car. Why can't I just keep this one?"

She must be teasing. At least I hope she is. I don't know for sure as I had promised to only speak to her through her mind, not to read it. "Because you are a classy woman."

"That I am, and Lamborghinis are classy."

The way she stretches out the word classy makes it obvious she is teasing me. A tinge of fear hits me as she tosses the Lamborghini keys to the valet and swaggers into the hotel just like Tad would. I guess she has seen him in enough movies to nail his attitude. A doorman opens the door for her, and she vanishes for a second as my viewer switches to the famous lobby of the Polo Lounge. It screams classic Hollywood with its walnut paneling polished to a high shine and the name Polo Lounge emblazoned on a bronze plaque like it is a historic monument, which in a way it is.

The host, dressed in a perfectly tailored black suit,

gives Tad a broad smile. "Good evening, sir. Mrs. Pearson is waiting for you. Let me take you to your booth."

Fiona says nothing, just nods and follows the host as he strides into the main part of the restaurant. He leads her to one of the large circular striped booths that rim the left side of the restaurant. The forest green and white striped ceiling and the rich green walls scream old school chic. So does the abundance of foliage in planters rimming the wall giving it an outdoor feel to match the patio beyond.

Rene stands up as soon as she sees who she thinks is Tad. She's wearing a skintight jersey dress in emerald green to match the décor. Her dark brunette hair is pulled back in a severe chignon. She looks like the former starlet she is. Rene's succubus identity remains hidden from even me. She has disguised her aura as human.

She kisses Tad smack on the mouth and pushes her ample bosom into his chest. How Fiona doesn't flitch is beyond me. She is proving herself to be the consummate professional even in this uncomfortable situation.

Fiona sits down in the booth keeping a bit of distance from Rene. "Oh, I see you have my martini waiting for me."

Rene nods. "If it's not cold enough, I can get you another."

Fiona shakes her head and downs half the drink. "It's like bathtub water, just the way I like it."

Rene nudges Fiona's ample bicep. "You do love to tease me so."

Fiona downs the rest of the drink and Rene signals the hovering waiter for another one. "So how has the read-through been going? I will miss you when you leave for Borneo."

"It's going good. Trish is a newbie, but we have good chemistry."

Fiona sounds just like Tad, every word laced in sarcasm.

Rene snarls. "How many sex scenes do you have with her? You know her body has been totally created by Dr. Wiseman."

I thought I'd heard of catty women, but Rene is an Olympic Gold medal level of bitch.

Fiona shrugs. "We have three." Her eye's narrow in on Rene's ample cleavage. "Don't be jealous. You still have the best tits in Hollywood."

If Fiona gets tired of being a detective for WI-6 she should become an actress.

Rene bats her eyelashes. "You are such a tease. My offer is still open."

Fiona gives her a wink. "Don't tempt me." She takes a sip of the fresh martini the waiter delivers. "So, have you gotten over the whole Grump incident? You sounded pretty upset when it happened."

Rene leans back in the booth and pushes away what is left of her strawberry daiquiri. "I feel bad for Max of course. But all the hours I put into seducing Buddy turned out to be a total waste. He won't even see me. I'm too much of a reminder of that night."

Fiona nods. "Understandable. Have you heard anything about from the police about his death? Was it natural or not?"

She shakes her head. "No, but I told you I have a feeling a paranormal was involved somehow. I could sense when I held Max in my arms; real magic took him. It was not a heart attack."

Fiona fights to keep a calm face. "Interesting. I guess the Order will be able to figure it out."

Rene huffs. "The Order? Why are you bringing them up? I had no idea you knew about them."

Crap. Rene doesn't know Tad is a demi-god.

Fiona fidgets with the cocktail napkin. "Derrick told me."

"Well, he should know all about the Order, he's one of them."

I pop into Fiona's mind. "Go to the restroom. I'll get Tad over here before Rene figures out she's been played."

Fiona excuses herself and I send Tad a frantic text. *"Dude, get over to the lounge ASAP. Rene is giving my shifter girlfriend a hard time. I want her to eat her words."*

I enter Fiona's mind. "Things are going south fast. Hang out in the bathroom. I'll signal you when Tad shows up."

Fiona walks into a stall in the men's room and closes the door. "Thank you so much. I don't know how much longer I could sit across from that dragon and not transform into an alligator so I could eat her."

I've never heard Fiona so mad. But I have a feeling Rene has that effect on everyone.

Tad finally responds. "Okay, buddy. I'll be there in a jiff."

And sure enough, he is. Demi-god magic is a mystery to me, but they obviously have transportation skills like the Twelfth Order. Even more impressive is the transport was seamless. No flashing lights or energy source announcing his arrival. Just one minute Tad wasn't at the lounge, the next he strolls out of the restroom and straight toward Rene's table. I've had enough Rene Pearson for one night.

Snapping my fingers, the viewing screen disappears. Exhausted from Fiona's close call with Rene, all I want to do is get home and crash in my bed. My phone buzzing this late tells me my plan may have to be on hold. I look at the number that seems vaguely familiar. Then a pang of memory hits me—it's Eshe. Again, the hairs on the back of my neck stand at attention knowing her call is not to catch up and talk about old times.

"Hi, Eshe, so good to hear from you. I hope you and Brooklyn are doing well."

Her beautiful Egyptian-accented voice comes through the speakers. "We are doing quite well, but someone close to you may not be in the near future."

I swallow hard. "Have you seen something in the caldron?"

"Yes, when the coven summoned Cherwin tonight. She had a very specific message for you. We need to meet to discuss what she said. Do you have any time tomorrow?"

"I'll make time. I can meet you in the morning, just name the hour."

"Nine o'clock. Bring your shifter partner. She's in danger."

7

COVEN CONFESSIONS

Fiona's eyes travel over the spectacle that is Eshe's living room. Her mouth opens slightly as she takes in the home's interior, which is a sharp contrast to the cookie cutter exterior. Eshe, who is a powerful high priestess, chose to lay low in the Valley instead of her Norwegian rival, who has a high-profile Frank Lloyd inspired mansion in Topanga Canyon as her coven headquarters.

Eshe greets Fiona with a warm smile wearing one of her signature gold caftans. "Welcome to my home."

Fiona gives her a slight bow as if Eshe is a minor royal. "Thank you for inviting me."

I give Eshe a weak smile, acknowledging she received my text where I explained I didn't have the heart to tell Fiona the real reason we came.

A squeal sounds behind me, followed by the sound of flapping wings. Brooklyn, Eshe's daughter, races toward me, her arms held out for a hug. "Oh, Derrick, it's been too long." Her eyes grow wet. "I still can't believe she's gone."

I hug Brooklyn tight. The bond of grief between us over the loss of Tara still seems as strong as ever. Tara was my fiancée, but she was like an older sister to Brooklyn and her favorite coven member.

We release each other and Brooklyn turns to Fiona who stands awkwardly, taking in the artfully draped sari fabric hanging down from the ceiling. Large wood panels framed by colorful saris have words in ancient Egyptian only Eshe can read.

Brooklyn holds out her hand to Fiona. "I'm Brooklyn, Derrick and I go way back. He's like the older brother I never had."

Fiona gives Brooklyn a sincere smile. "It's good to meet you. Derrick has spoken highly of you and your mother."

She squeezes Fiona's hand. "Let me introduce you to the rest of the coven."

The coven and their menagerie of animal familiars are seated on embroidered cushions scattered all over the living room floor. She leads her over to Shana and her red fox familiar. "This is Shana, and next to her is Glenda."

Glenda looks far different than the last time I saw her. We had dated for a while until I fell in love with Tara. I loved Glenda's free spirit, bouncy curls, and charming Southern accent but we weren't serious. She looks up at me with her big blue eyes framed by long perfectly straight hair. I can't tell if the change in her hair is from magic or liberal use of a straightening device.

"Derrick good to see you. I'm glad it's under much better circumstances."

The irony of her words isn't lost on me. We last saw each other at Tara's funeral. But I don't think a death threat on my new girlfriend is much of an improvement. "Great to see you. Love the hair."

She beams and runs her hands through her silky blonde straight hair. "Sometimes a girl wants a change."

Fiona has no idea what she used to look like but smiles and says, "It suits you."

Brooklyn chimes in, "Enough of the love fest, I'd like you to meet our newest coven member, "Tanith, she is my cousin from Egypt."

She is shorter than Eshe and has a less voluptuous figure, but the family resemblance of high cheekbones and a long, elegant nose is obvious. "Nice to meet you," he says in a beautiful accent similar to Eshe's. "A pleasure to meet you. I've heard much about the mysterious dark-haired wizard of the Twelfth Order."

My mind reels with all the stories she could have heard about me, yet I simply smile. "Why, thank you. I hope I will live up to my reputation."

A chuckle comes from the bat familiar resting on Brooklyn's shoulder. In his snooty British accent he says, "Good to see you, Derrick. You don't look too much worse for wear."

Fred is as snarky as ever. Yet, I am forever grateful

for him saving Tara's life when the vampires attacked her the first time. "I wish I could have come to Tara's aid during the second attack. I am terribly sorry."

There was nothing any of us could do. We had no idea the Tara's life was in danger as we thought all the evil vampires in Murdock's clan had been killed.

"I know you would have done something if you could, Fred."

Eshe claps her hands together and signals for me to stand by her side. "Let us begin the meeting." She turns to me. "Can you retrieve the cauldron, Derrick?"

A pang of pain hits me. The last time I played my role of cauldron totter, Tara was alive and well. Brooklyn gets Fiona settled onto a floor cushion next to her while I head off to the kitchen to get the cauldron. Brooklyn always teased about why, as a wizard of the Twelfth Order, I never used my powerful magic to move the cauldron. As I rarely make it to the gym, it is a great way to get a good bicep work out.

Pulling the cauldron out of its hiding place in the laundry room next to the dryer, I take in the pretty green retro tile in the kitchen and flashback to when Tara would tickle me and try to get me to drop the cauldron. The memory doesn't hurt quite as much as I thought. In fact, I find a faint smile on my face. Tara's sense of humor was one of the things I loved about her. Fiona doesn't have her playfulness, but I have grown up a lot since my days with Tara. I think someone sensible and reliable like Fiona is what I need at this time in my life.

Just like a weightlifter, I take a big deep breath, bend my knees, and pick up the cauldron. I turn the corner into the small dining room with ease and place the cauldron in the center of the living room in front of the ring of floor cushions.

Sitting down on the empty floor cushion next to Fiona, I fight back the memory of Tara sitting next to me and squeezing my hand. I should have known coming back to Eshe's home for the first time after the wake would cause an avalanche of memories, good and bad. Eshe stands before us looking like a vision as the ceiling lights aim right at her gold caftan, making her whole body sparkle. She tosses her long dark hair over her shoulders and says, "We are here to summon Cherwin again. Please put your hands together and concentrate on the cauldron while I summon the goddess."

The instructions are only for the benefit of Fiona. The coven is well versed in how to summon the goddess who can see the future. Eshe takes a few bunches of herbs from a black velvet pouch she pulls out of her voluminous caftan. With the grace of a conductor with their wand, Eshe tosses the herbs into the cauldron, and it begins to bubble furiously. She chants in an ancient Egyptian tongue and the bubbling stops abruptly. A strange golden glow emanates from the center of the cauldron, and I hear a slight gasp from Fiona's lips. I reach over and give her hand a reassuring squeeze. Dating a wizard isn't for lightweights, especially one of the Twelfth Order. We seem to have our hand in countless aspects of the paranormal world and have many magical allies like the witches of Eshe's coven.

Eshe runs her hand through the golden glow, and it undulates like Jell-O.

A woman's Irish voice floats through the air. "You summoned me?" Then the image of a woman with long flowing blond hair artfully draped over a pleated gossamer gown comes into view.

"Yes, Cherwin, the great goddess of the future. The last time our coven summoned you, you heeded a warning to a shifter that is close to someone in the coven. Someone from near the land of your birth."

Fiona's brow furrows not understanding that Eshe made me an honoree member of her coven.

At first there is silence, then Cherwin says, "Yes, although I now realize the shifter's country of origin is southern Asia."

Fiona bites her lip, knowing Cherwin is talking about her."

Eshe nods and gives a slight bow to Cherwin. "The shifter you mentioned is present. What is your warning to her?"

Cherwin's light Irish lilt deepens. "The warning is twofold. The Asian shifter is in danger from one of her own kind. The rival shifter is threatened by her skills. This shifter is also deeply resentful of wizards of the Twelfth Order as they have discovered the shifter's existence. The shifter plans to retaliate by taking away the people the Twelfth Order wizards love."

Although Cherwin's message is dire, I fight back the urge to cheer. She has revealed the evil shifter's link to my mission for the Order. If I can find the shifter, then I can solve my mission and quit Zoomer duty. I could get my life back, having only to do one job.

With Cherwin's message delivered she sinks back into the cauldron. The gold glow shutters and disappears.

Eshe looks down at Fiona. "I did not mean to scare you at our first meeting." She holds her arms open, taking in the coven sitting before her. "We are here to help you, Fiona. Sisters, please put your hands together and we shall cast a protection spell to ward off the evil shifter."

I hold hands with Brooklyn, who takes Shana's, and Glenda's hand. Eshe closes her eyes and chants in her ancient language. Fiona's shoulders stiffen as the protection surges through her body.

When the coven breaks hands, Fiona looks up at Eshe with awe. "I felt something wash over me like a warm hug."

Eshe smiles. "That is a wonderful description of the spell. It is the energy from all of us and our ancestors. It should stave off your enemy."

Fiona shivers at the sound of the word but says nothing.

Eshe turns her gaze to me. "I will give you a hex bag to boost your protection spell, Derrick."

A velvet bag levitates from where the book of

shadows is stored, and drifts toward me, and then rests at my feet.

I smile when I see Fiona's large dark eyes grow even larger. With admiration in her eyes, she looks up at Eshe. "I don't know how I can thank you and your coven for the warning and for the protection spell."

Eshe smiles down on Fiona. "Stay alive."

AFTER AN EMOTIONALLY DRAINING MORNING WITH the coven, checking into WI-6 headquarters can only be described as mundane. Even more so when we find *The Pit* totally empty.

Fiona sits down at her desk. "What is going on? Not even Mr. Pierre is here. I'm going to check the WI-6 private email and see if we missed a memo."

It does seem odd that not even Ms. Burke, the office manager and sleuth in training, is running around trying to tie up loose ends we detectives leave behind.

Fiona taps her screen. "I was right. Mr. Pierre sent out a memo that a crew of technicians were coming to *The Pit* today, so we are to work from home."

As if on cue a loud clatter sounds from above us. Talk about over kill. Mr. Pierre already had almost every square inch of *The Pit* bugged. Could he be up to something even more sinister? I don't want to stick around to find out. We will both be reprimanded if we are caught. "Fiona, we need to hightail it out of here."

A big burly guy saunters into the room wearing a

pair of dusty blue overalls with a patch above the pocket that says, *WI Secret Service.*

I try not to laugh as he strides into the office and gets right up in my face. "I was told no one would be here. Who are you?"

Fiona gets up out of her chair and stands next to the burly tech guy. "I'm so sorry. We missed the memo not to come into work this morning." She loops her arm around mine. "We are leaving."

She pulls me toward the door and the burly guy shouts after us, "I'm going to tell Mr. Pierre you were here."

TAKING FIONA'S HAND, WE WALK INTO THE PATIO area of the Chateau Marmont, hoping to put a more than eventful day behind us. I feel like the luckiest man at the party having Fiona by my side. She is wearing a stunning deep peacock blue sari trimmed in silver embroidery. It clings to her body like Saran Wrap. I whisper in her ear, "You take my breath away, and by the looks of all the glances you are getting, I think I'm not the only one."

She squeezes my hand. "I wanted to make an impression on the Los Angeles elite, and you."

I push her hair off her shoulder exposing her neck and dive in for a kiss."

"Get a room," shouts a familiar voice moving toward us. Krissy is weaves her way through a series of large potted trees edging the patio. It resembles a checkerboard made up of alternating squares of grass and concrete paving stones.

Krissy is making quite the impression herself wearing a skintight red lycra dress. Her long blonde hair is pulled up in a high ponytail to reveal a plunging back that stops above her tailbone. "You two look quite stunning together."

Fiona holds out her hand, her silver bangles making a pretty, bell-like sound. "I'm Fiona, and you must be Krissy."

"Oh, my gosh. Your voice is as beautiful as you are."

I need to break up the gush fest. "Krissy has a thing for Brits."

She smacks my bicep. "So what, they have wonderful speaking voices. We Americans sound like nails on a blackboard."

Fiona chuckles. "I think that might be a slight exaggeration."

Krissy looks at me sternly. "If you let this one, get away, I will personally come over to your house and give you the thrashing of your life."

Fiona smiles at me and gives Krissy a wink. "I like the friends you keep."

I put my hands up like I'm defending myself from an imminent assault. "I surrender." Then I place my arm around Fiona's waist and say, "Don't worry, Krissy, I know she's a keeper."

A tall, handsome man wearing an impeccably tailored tuxedo who looks like the actor who played the

Duke in the TV series *Bridgeton* walks up behind Krissy and covers her eyes. "Guess who?"

Turns out he has the voice to match, a very deep British baritone.

She whirls around and smiles up at the man. "The star of the evening. And where is your stunning wife?"

He glances toward the main section of the hotel. "Being the consummate hostess."

He gives Fiona and I a discerning glance. "And this must be the couple you begged me to invite to the party." He holds out his pale hand to me. "Krissy has spoken highly of you, Derrick."

I shake his hand, wondering just how much Krissy has told him about me. After shaking his hand and reading his aura, I know Shoran is a powerful vampire king. "I hope she didn't puff me up too much. I do appreciate the invitation to your party."

Shoran chuckles. "You know Krissy, she puffs everyone up, including herself."

Fiona gives me a slight nudge. "And may I introduce my girlfriend, Fiona."

Shoran takes in her beautiful face. "Welcome to Los Angeles. Krissy tells me you are a recent transplant from the UK. Welcome to the expat club."

"Yes, I am," Fiona says as she reaches down and holds my hand. "Turns out I'm old fashioned and followed my man across the pond."

Shoran gives me a look of admiration. "You are a lucky man." Then he looks past us and smiles and waves. "I am as well."

A woman that can only be described as a Selma Hayek body double moves toward us, her dark hair brushing her bare shoulder and her hips swaying back and forth in almost a samba-like rhythm. In an accent that is like her doppelganger she says, "Krissy, is this the couple you were telling me about? I could feel their power across the room."

Interesting. Shoran is a vampire, but his wife is a succubus. Her aura is unmistakable. An odd couple in the paranormal world to say the least. But it explains her powerful sexual energy. She holds out her hand. "Happy to meet you. I'm Catalina. You must be Derrick, the special person I've heard so much about. It is not often I get to meet a wizard of the Twelfth Order."

Catalina strokes my ego for all it's worth. "Why, thank you. And thank you for allowing us to attend this amazing party."

She finally glances at Fiona. "Your sari is quite beautiful. It suits you well."

"Thank you. I'm Fiona. I hope you don't mind my asking, but are you from Argentina? There is something in your accent that sounds familiar."

If Fiona is trying to impress Catalina it is not going to work. A succubus must always be the queen bee.

"Close. I am from Chile."

Fiona takes the rebuff in stride. "My mistake."

Sensing some growing tension between the women, Shoran says, "Why don't we join a group of my friends in the lobby area? I had the hotel set up a small bar if you would like a drink."

Shoran and Catalina lock arms and head into the hotel while we hang back a minute to wait for Krissy.

She loops her arm in mine. "Aren't they the most amazing power couple?"

"Yes, indeed." I lead the women toward the lobby, working our way around a small group of Hollywood beautiful people and walk past two huge sets of curtains and into the main part of the hotel. "They are powerful indeed. It appears they have rented the entire hotel for the evening."

Krissy nods. "They did. Shoran has quite the fortune."

Most vampire kings do if they manage to live long enough. Every nerve in my body tingles at the thought that once again a vampire king has entered my life. At least this time he isn't trying to kill everyone I love. I sense no ill will from him—at least for now.

Fiona reaches over and holds my hand. She can sense that I am on edge. I give her a smile, happy we are forming a special bond together. "I'll be alright."

She whispers in my ear. "It's because he is a vampire king, isn't it?"

Fiona read his aura too. "I'll be fine. Let's enjoy the evening."

Krissy strides ahead of us oblivious to the anger I'm fighting to control. I shouldn't expect her to understand. Krissy met me after Tara died and I was numb to the world. We were typical surface Los Angeles friends.

I never once in all our Zoomer rides together told her the true story of Tara. Krissy just knew about her death through the paranormal grapevine.

We enter the grand lobby of the hotel and, like the time when Fiona caught her first glimpse of Eshe's eclectic living room, she lets out a tiny gasp as she takes in the old Hollywood glamour of the hotel. The large lobby is an eclectic mix of regal overstuffed furniture and beautiful antiques. The enormous Spanish wrought iron chandeliers hover over us like huge black crowns.

"The place looks like a movie set."

I chuckle knowing at least forty movies have been filmed at Chateau Marmont. "It has been in quite a few films over the decades. Two of the most recent were big box office hits, *La La Land* and *A Star is Born* with Lady Gaga."

Fiona looks a bit star struck. "No wonder it looks vaguely familiar."

I spot Shoran talking with his friends who are all vampires and decide I need a drink. "Do you mind if I hit the bar? I need to take the edge off."

Fiona follows my gaze. "It appears a lot of his clan are here. I think a large drink is in order."

Once again, she reads my emotions well. It makes me want to take her home and jump into that new bed of hers. But I sense this evening is an important one, so I know I must stay.

At the bar I order a whiskey on the rocks and Fiona takes a glass of champagne. She rubs the back of my neck. "Ignore the vampires. We don't want to disappoint Krissy."

I nod knowing she is right. Downing my whiskey, I feel the warmth of the liquor slide down my throat, easing my nerves ever so slightly.

A slight whoosh of air makes me turn around. Shoran stands next to me, his piercing dark eyes scrutinizing me, but he does not enter my mind. "Rough day?"

His vampire speed is impressive. He made it across the lobby in seconds. "I'll say. It's been non-stop since I woke up."

He smiles. "I know how you feel. My day has been hectic as well. I learned something that actually may be of interest to you."

Shoran reminds me of Mr. Kumar and The Exemplary Wizard rolled into one. They too love to stretch out their words to add to the suspense of what they have to say. "Can you tell me now?"

He looks around the room and shakes his head. "Not here. Meet me tomorrow at my offices on Wilshire Boulevard at 10:00 AM. I think we may have a common foe that must be extinguished."

8

TURNS OUT VAMPIRES CAN BE ALLIES

After dropping Fiona off at her place, I know what I must do. I press the auto dial on my screen for the one person who will understand the significance of what I learned at the party—Mr. Kumar.

The phone rings and clicks over to voicemail. I shouldn't expect to reach him at this time of night. It's when he has meetings with the Exemplary Wizard.

Driving away from Fiona's apartment, exhaustion washes over me. I'm glad my bungalow is only a few blocks away. Just as I pull up into my driveway, a familiar voice enters my head. "It must be something important for you to leave such an exciting party."

Mr. Kumar couldn't resist getting a little mindreading in. "It is, sir. I'm happy to announce I no longer need to work my job as a Zoomer driver."

"So, you have identified the troublemaking shifter?"

"Not exactly, sir. But I know someone who is just as eager to find out who they are."

Mr. Kumar drifts out of my mind and then back again. He must have had a final comment for the Exemplary Wizard. "Are you sure you can work with a vampire king after what happened with Murdock?"

Mind reading again. "Yes, sir. Shoran seems quite different from Murdock. I sense no ill will from him even though he has a block on his mind."

"Interesting how the vampire kings always have a witch to cast spells for them."

"He seems to have an affection for wizards. Perhaps Shoran has a wizard under retainer instead of a witch."

"That's an interesting prospect. Most wizards abhor vampires, but I have no prejudice against them. They have given me no cause other than Murdock and his clan."

This is something about Mr. Kumar I never knew. He has worked with vampires before. "I have a meeting with him tomorrow morning and believe working together we will find the renegade shifter. Of course, I still have a case to solve for WI-6, but somehow I sense that case will be resolved soon."

Mr. Kumar laughs. "You aren't getting cocky after solving two cases, are you?"

He's sounding more like a father than my boss. Which I don't mind, as my own father had no enthusiasm for my desire to be a wizard. Baggage from growing up with a father who was second in command of the Twelfth Order in Chicago. "Don't worry, sir, I know I'm still a newbie detective and a juvenile wizard of the Twelfth Order."

A hearty laugh fills my mind. "I think you are a bit further down the wizard path than that. I'd say at least a young adult."

My turn to laugh at my expense. "Why thank you, sir."

"Thank you for reporting in with some good news for a change. Give me a call or pop in after your morning meeting."

I love the fact when we wizards say we might pop in, we are talking about minds not homes. "Of course, sir. Hopefully we can apprehend the shifter soon."

"I hope so because they have been causing quite a bit of havoc. They seem to have a grudge against wizards."

A chill runs down my back. Cherwin's prediction is coming true.

WHILE FIONA IS AT WI-6 HEADQUARTERS interviewing more possible suspects and witnesses in the Grump case, I'm standing in front of a nondescript brown stone and glass building, one of several off Wilshire Boulevard. Ironically it is only two blocks away from the La Brea Tar Pits, which was the hideout for Murdock, the last vampire king I dealt with. I like that Shoran has chosen a location hidden in plain sight for his clans' headquarters. Like Eshe and her cookie cutter tract home headquarters, it shows he is smart and has no desire to call attention to himself. The polar opposite of Murdock, who was as flamboyant as they come. His headquarters was in the depths of the La Brea Tar Pit Museum. Although I should have expected such an outrageous choice from a vampire who gained his power during the Victorian age and pretended to be a Lord related to the royal family.

I walk past a sterile concrete courtyard, the only hint of color coming from the neatly trimmed box hedges forming squares inside a large white concrete planter. There is nothing fancy in this office complex unlike where the WI-6 headquarters is located. I enter the lobby area that has no guard and face a bank of elevators. This morning, Shoran texted me the name of his company, Energy Source. I find the name on the directory and smile at the fact it is written in red. Energy source equals blood. Unlike Ainsley, the artist vampire, whose energy source comes from taking memories of animals thanks to a spell, Shoran and his clan are traditional and use blood.

Pushing the button for the 4th floor, I have no feeling of dread that the blood that courses through my veins will be the source of energy for Shoran. One thing about experienced creatures in the paranormal world, we have a mutual respect for one another. One hard earned over many centuries of wars and rivalries.

The elevator door opens onto a floor with five vampires all dressed in black using their extreme speed to move about the office in mere seconds. The light is dim, yet it is obvious Shoran's wizard has cast a spell so that sunlight is not a problem for them.

A tall brunette woman wearing a black dress and a red lipstick smile and moves toward me. "Hello Mr. Dunne. I am Shoran's assistant, Velma. He is running a bit late, so he asked me to take you into his office. Would you like a coffee and a croissant? They are the kind with chocolate in the middle."

"That would be much appreciated. I ran out of the house without breakfast."

She snaps her fingers and a redhead girl also dressed in black races toward the back corner of the floor. Velma has a deliberate stride as she leads me past several meeting rooms and to a large office with a view of the spartan courtyard. "Make yourself at home. Shoran says he will be here in five."

Just as with wizards, vampires can communicate through their minds. Unless they have had a witch or wizard to cast a protection spell that blocks access as I have done. I admit I much prefer the human way of communicating through texting and by phone. Entering someone's mind can be a jarring experience and if you are not careful; their thoughts and memories can be overwhelming.

The redheaded assistant leads me into an executive office with a view of the Art Museum. The décor is an interesting mix of glass, black leather and ebony wood floors. A large glass desk takes center stage.

One of the other vampires arrives, carrying a silver tray with a pot of coffee, tea and sugar and the chocolate croissant on a gold-rimmed china dessert plate. She places it on a small glass table next to a black modern leather chair. "Enjoy."

Shoran sure is a class act but he is British and upper crust, so I shouldn't be surprised. I pour my coffee, put in a splash of cream, and take a big sip. Then I take a huge bit of the warm croissant and the chocolate oozes out of the corners, giving me two dark streaks on either side of my mouth.

Before I can wipe them off Shoran strides in, sits behind his glass desk and starts to laugh. "You seem to be enjoying the croissant a trifle too much."

Pulling the cloth napkin from the tray, I clean up the chocolate. "It is delicious. I swear it tastes like the ones I've had at a patisserie in Paris."

He beams. "You have discriminating taste. I have them flown in fresh every day from La Barouche."

Of course he does. When Krissy said he had a fortune, my original estimate was he had a multi-million empire. After taking in his headquarters, I need to change it to a billionaire. "Nothing like getting French food from the source."

He leans back in his leather executive chair. "Indeed. I know this is going to sound odd coming from a vampire, but life is short one should enjoy the things that give one pleasure."

I flash back to Murdock and his bloody death at the hands of Jennifer in the form of a Saber Tooth Tiger and know he is right. "We are gifted with long lives, but we are not immortal."

Shoran gives me a weak smile. "We are off to a cracking start, aren't we?"

I laugh. "It isn't often I get a chance to sit back and have a frank conversation with a vampire."

The redhead comes bounding in with a wine glass on a silver tray. To the non-discerning eye, someone would think it is just a glass of red wine, but I know it is a glass of blood, but not human.

Shoran catches me eyeing the glass. "It is my favorite cocktail of claret, grenadine, and sheep's blood. I am not like your friend, vampire Ainsley. But truth be told if I did know a witch who could cast a spell to free me of the blood energy source, I would still partake of it. I like the distinctive flavor."

I shouldn't be surprised a vampire king would be a bit of a blood connoisseur, yet somehow, I am. Holding up my coffee cup I say, "To the energy source of ones choosing."

He holds his wine glass up high. "Here, here," and then downs half the glass. Still a bit hungry, I polish off the rest of the croissant while Shoran finishes his blood cocktail. "I'm grateful you wish to work with me on the shifter problem."

Shoran runs his tongue over his teeth and then smiles. Not a trace of blood insight. "I like the American saying, *two heads are better than one*. It is quite true. I promise anything you tell me will be in the strictest confidence I will tell no one including my wife."

Unfortunately, I can't make the same promise. I must keep Fiona in the loop as she is one of only a few paranormals who can unmask the shifter. "Of course, I will do the same except for two exceptions. The shifter is wanted by the Order as they seem to have a grudge against wizards especially from the Twelfth Order. I also must tell a shifter who will be able to aid us in unmasking the rogue shifter."

He nods. "I understand. The fact that you have a shifter you trust at your disposal is wonderful news. Of course, the upper echelon of the Order reigns above us all."

Letting out a chuckle, I say, "Truer words have never been spoken." I hold out my hand. "Let's shake on it."

Shoran gives me a normal, firm handshake. The only hint that he is a vampire is the slight translucence to his skin and how it is cool to the touch.

He sits back down in his chair. "As I invited you here, I will tell you what I know first."

I nod and open the note taking spell in my mind. "I hope you don't mind if I take notes."

His brow furrows. "We do not allow recording devices. Our voices are quite distinctive as you know."

Vampires' voices have a low undertone that only paranormals can hear. Yet there is a fear that the human vampire hunters will one day manage to get a recording and when they analyze it, they will hear the distinctive sound too. Then the vampires will be revealed when they speak.

"Have no fear. I have a dictation spell that notes everything you say and stores it in my memory."

A wry smile crosses his lips. "The wonders of the Twelfth Order magic never cease to amaze me."

"I can't take credit for the spell. My boss cast it."

"Please tell him I am impressed with his magic the next time you see him. I believe we paranormals should compliment each other's skills at every opportunity."

Shoran is quickly becoming my second favorite vampire after Ainsley. "It would be my pleasure. It's a wonderful sentiment to live by."

He smiles. "And now that our mutual admiration festivities are over, let's get down to business. We first were made aware of the rogue shifter when he impersonated my second in command. He took several liberties that could have compromised him and possibly gotten him killed."

Rogue wizards running around causing havoc for the Order is nothing new to me. Finding them was part of my reconnaissance job. But this is the first time I have heard of a rogue shifter. Usually, they are quite solitary, like succubi. They tended to only use their skills when necessary for their survival. To use the shifting skill for kicks was unheard of until now. Shifters like Fiona and Jennifer are nothing like their animal shifter cousins, like Krissy.

"I don't know what to say but I'm sorry to hear the news. Working for the Order to control wayward wizards has been hard enough. Dealing with a rogue shifter is going to be beyond tricky. My friend is going to be vital in tracking this villain down."

"Yes, I am so glad you have an ally in the shifter

world. I am aware that they have a distinct aura like all paranormals, but I've never seen one in the flesh."

"They can hide their aura from us with the aid of a wizard or a witch, but they can never mask themselves from each other. At least we have that going for us."

Shoran temples his hands on his desk. "Will you protect the identity of your shifter ally with a spell?"

It seems he is one step ahead of me. A high priestess has already given Fiona a powerful protection spell. I must add an indent concealment spell on top of it. "Of course. A coven has already graced the shifter with a powerful protection spell, as the high priestess found out the shifter was in danger."

"Good. We must ask your shifter friend to put themselves at risk several times to catch the rogue."

I know he is right. My hands grow clammy at the thought of Fiona being used as bait. But we had to do the same thing with Jennifer to catch Murdock. "I have another duty I must juggle as well as catching the rogue, but I promise you if you send me a lead, I will drop everything."

He un-temples his fingers and looks me straight in the eye with his hypnotic gaze. "I have one request."

"Of course, anything."

"When you find the shifter, I would like the honor of bleeding them dry."

CRUISING DOWN THE 405 FREEWAY HEADING TO WI-6 headquarters, I'm just about to let Fiona know I'm heading her way when a text from her pops up on my screen. *"Meet me in a half an hour at North Spring Street and Baker. I had an interesting conversation with the hostess at Mr. Grump's favorite bar, the Acropolis. I think you Americans like to say watering hole. If my gut is right, she might have important information about the death by beer case."*

Just like Fiona to bust her butt and get our case back on track. I'd been feeling guilty constantly sidelining the case. The Grumps deserved better. Yet, I am optimistic that with the help of Shoran, the rogue shifter will soon be dealt with.

As I drive toward central Los Angeles, I can see the bar is near Dodger Stadium. Getting off the freeway, I know surface streets are going to be far quicker as it's lunch time. I finally hit Sunset and my phone buzzes through on the screen. "How did your meeting go with the vampire king?"

Mr. Kumar must have let his curiosity get the better of him. Normally he would wait until I called him. "Good. I think the shifter's time is numbered. Shoran is quite ticked as he posed as his second in command and apparently caused quite the problem."

Mr. Kumar sounding quite indignant being a second in command himself, says, "That is a violation of the highest order."

"It is, which certainly works in our favor."

"True. How is your beer case going?"

It's nice of him to care about my WI-6 job. "Not

good. Too many distractions. But Fiona has made some headway."

"Splendid. Well, I won't keep you any longer."

A loud click ends the conversation. Mr. Kumar's time is a precious thing. I truly appreciate his fatherly concern about me. Pulling up to the Acropolis Bar, I decide to cast a protection spell on my Beemer. With no Holmes to fend burglars off, I have little choice in what looks like a sketchy neighborhood. The outside of the bar is your typical non-descript brick storefront from the thirties or forties. Pulling open the ocean blue door my eyes must adjust quickly to the almost dungeon-like lighting. It's not as dark as *The Pit* because the back wall is taken up by a spectacular onyx stone bar that is lit from underneath. Every pattern in the stone is highlighted, creating a spectacular work of art.

Fiona stands at the end of the bar, chatting with a girl wearing a bohemian floral dress made up of blues and purples. Her dress works well with the funky decor of the bar. A combination of boho chic with a nod to its ancient Greek name covers the back wall. It's punctuated by arches and columns painted a sandy gold color similar to the Acropolis.

Fiona smiles when she sees me. "Here he is. Derrick, meet Heidi."

No surnames. Fiona is going casual for this interview. "Nice to meet you. Thank you for agreeing to talk with us."

Heidi motions for us to take the seats next to her at the bar. "I was just telling Fiona I'm more than happy to help. I really liked Max. He was a regular and great guy. I couldn't believe he died. He drank a lot, but he seemed to handle it well."

Fiona nods. "Yes, we've heard he was a nice man and a talented magician. Buddy, his son, showed us the bottle trick. Truly amazing."

Heidi clapped her hands together. "Oh, that was one of my favorites. He always was so nice about performing tricks when people asked."

Fiona leans closer to Heidi. "You mentioned when I talked to you on the phone that you had an issue with the bartender about the same time as when Max passed."

"Yes, Brad was a bit squirrely the week before he died. He would ask to work certain days and then cancel. Then, somehow, he would show up. It was beyond strange. Normally Brad is super reliable. Then the week after Max died, he just up and quit."

The story was getting interesting. The bartender either had major personal problems or something more sinister might have been the explanation. "How long had he been working at the Acropolis?"

Heidi stared at one of the columns on the back bar wall. "Um." She rubs her temples as if that could pull up a memory. "I think he was here a year before me. So that means he had been working at the bar for almost three years."

Now it's getting interesting. "Was the owner shocked when he quit?"

"He was pissed! He sent Brad to a top bartending

school his first year. After that, he sent Brad to a special cocktail making course in Europe. My boss felt betrayed."

Fiona nods. "That sounds like a big investment in someone. I doubt he would have done it if he thought Brad would walk off the job one day."

"Of course not."

A question burned in the back of my mind. "Would you say Brad had a personality change before he left?"

Heidi's eyes grew wide. "I never thought about it before but, yes. Those two weeks he did almost seem like a different person. Yet, he looked the same, his walk was the same, but his jokes were slightly off. But the biggest thing that threw me off was the fact that he didn't seem interested in me anymore. Brad used to tease and flirt with me at least a couple times a night. But for those two weeks before Max died, he never flirted once. I brushed it off, thinking maybe he found someone, but he never seemed interested in dating, just playing around."

This is the news we've been waiting for. I'm too excited to wait to talk to Fiona after the interview. Instead, I enter her mind. "Excuse me for popping in, but I couldn't wait to see if you agree with me. Heidi's description of Brad's change in behavior makes me think of only one thing."

Fiona is startled at first to have me inside her mind, then she says, "The bartender was taken over by a shifter."

9

WHO IS BRAD THE BARTENDER?

Fiona knocks once and comes strolling in with Renoir on her heels. She is dressed in a blue, floral, body-hugging maxi wrap dress. She's not going to make this work dinner easy. I suppose I deserve it after busting into her mind with no warning.

She eyes the table set for two. A lone silver candle holder with a flickering candle stands smack dab in the center. "I thought this was a work dinner. It looks quite romantic."

Holmes chimes in. "Trust me it was an afterthought. He raced through the door and started snapping his fingers this way and that. Then another snap, the table was set."

Renoir sniffs the air. "Do I smell the distinct scent of oysters, figs, and duck, all cooked in the French style?"

I beam. "Yes, you do. I felt like a small four course

French meal was in order after a hard yet fulfilling day." I pull a chair out for Fiona. "I hope the meal will meet your expectations."

Renoir settles in by Fiona's feet. A bad habit she has surely learned from Holmes. He loves to beg for scraps when I eat at home. To prove I'm right, Holmes plops down next to my vacant chair, his long floppy ears draped on the hardwood floor.

Fiona decides to give me the silent treatment as she sits down in the chair. Then she points to a champagne glass next to her gold-rimmed china dinner plate. "Is this straight champagne?"

"No, it's a French 75. Why not conjure a special cocktail to celebrate the news that the shifter more than likely posed as the bartender at the Acropolis?"

She takes a small sip. "Oh, it's quite refreshing. It's a mix of lemon juice, gin, lavender, and champagne."

"Yes, and a splash of simple syrup. I'm glad you like it."

She looks down at the plate laden with six oysters on the half shell and a fig tart covered in dabs of melted goat cheese. "Oysters are an interesting choice. I thought you promised if you ever entered my mind, you wouldn't read it."

I swallow hard. Either they are a favorite or she's interested in testing out that new bed of hers. "I promise I did not read your mind. The oysters are a classic appetizer for the meal I conjured."

Her cheeks flush. "Oh, good."

Now I wish I had read her mind about her favorite

foods. Does she have some fantasy about us eating oysters and then making love? I sure hope so. I sit down in my chair and hold up my glass. "A toast to finally getting a good lead in the Grump case."

She smiles and we clink glasses. "Yes. I admit I had been getting worried after so many distractions and bad leads."

Fiona never told me about the bad leads, but I never totally explained my distractions either. "Bon appetit."

We both dig into the tart, taking breaks to eat an oyster or two. By the way the food is vanishing off dishes, it appears neither one of us had any lunch. The only thing I had for breakfast was the croissant at Shoran's office.

She dabs her mouth after polishing off the last oyster. "You conjure an excellent French meal. Did you use a favorite meal at a restaurant for inspiration?"

"Normally, I would, but this meal is composed of things I have a craving for."

"Brilliant so far. What is next?"

I snap my fingers and the dirty dishes disappear and two plates appear with the entrée.

"Oh, how marvelous. I love duck and cherries. The pea salad is such a wonderful complement, and so nicely presented as well."

Now I know Fiona has the same weakness for good food. She walked in quite angry, but now she seems to be warming up to me. My magical skills to the rescue yet again. I eye her almost empty glass. "Would you like another French 75?"

Her eyes narrow. "Are you trying to get me drunk so you can have your way with me?"

Holmes looks up from the large bone I conjured for him. "Derrick is an honorable man. He would never dream of doing such a thing."

Oh yes, I would, I think to myself. But Holmes defending my honor can't go unrewarded. "Holmes is correct. I was just being a good host." I snap my fingers and Holmes's bone is miraculously covered with meat again. He barks his appreciation.

Renoir looks up at Fiona. "If you could spare a piece of duck, it would be much appreciated. It is one of my favorites."

Two duck slices disappear off Fiona's plate and she places them in front of Renoir's paws. "There you go, girl. Enjoy."

Instead of gobbling them up in seconds like Holmes would do, Renoir takes dainty little bites. Her manners are the same as her mistress.

Fiona leans back and dabs the corners of her mouth with the cloth napkin I conjured. "You have outdone yourself, partner. This meal deserves three Michelin stars." She gives me a sly smile. "I've changed my mind. I think I'll have another French 75. What delight do you have planned for dessert?"

"Traditionally I know I should serve a plate of different cheeses next, but I have a special weakness for chocolate mousse." I snap my fingers and our dinner plates vanish, and in their place sit two white porcelain cups on matching saucers. They are filled to the brim with mousse.

"First the oysters, then the cocktail, and now chocolate mousse? Are you certain you aren't trying to weaken my defenses?"

I snap my fingers again and two French 75s appears on the table. "We've been working hard I don't see why we can't indulge ourselves a little."

She tosses her long hair over her shoulders and takes a big sip of the drink. "You're right. It's nice to finally relax." Then she reaches over and squeezes my hand. "Thank you for the lovely meal, and I do feel completely relaxed, but isn't this supposed to be a working dinner?"

I'm really off my game. Here I conjured the perfect romantic meal, and we are supposed to be working. At least I got Fiona to relax.

Holmes looks up from the bone he's managed to pick clean again. "Yes, I distinctly remember this was supposed to be a working dinner."

Seems my attempt to change it to something else is an epic failure. I devour a big spoonful of the chocolate mousse as if it can sooth my bruised ego. "Do you have someone else lined up to interview tomorrow? Although I think the hostess is hard to beat."

As Fiona smiles, a tiny line of chocolate mousse is coating her two front teeth. "Actually, I do."

I force down a laugh as the chocolate lingers. "Who have you lined up?"

"The bartender, Brad. I put Ms. Burke on the case and once again she has proved to be excellent at sleuthing."

I lean back in my chair a bit taken back that Ms. Burke would help us after we caused her to be put on leave. Of course, it was for her misconduct. "That is wonderful news. Do we know if we will be interviewing the real Brad or the shifter posing as Brad?"

She beams. "That is for you to find out."

I smile knowing I have a surprise for her too. "I like a challenge. And I have one for you as well."

Her perfectly arched eyebrows rise. "Really? Something bigger than the wonderful meal you conjured?"

"All I will say is that it is something I promised to do for you, and I am finally delivering." I motion for her to stand up. "Follow me."

She pats Renoir on the head. "I'll be right back, girl."

Then she follows me out the back door and into the garage. Normally I would open the main garage door, but I want to keep her in suspense a bit longer. "Close your eyes."

She quickly does as I ask. "You sure are building up the suspense."

I clap my hands and the garage light pops on. Taking her by the hand, I lead her into the garage. Gently moving her in front of me until she is perfectly aligned with the surprise, I say, "Open your eyes."

She lets out a gasp. "Oh, my heavens. It's a Tesla S

model, and it's painted my favorite color, dark peacock blue."

Fiona throws her arms around me and gives me the deep passionate kiss I've been longing for. We kiss for a long time and then I hear scratching at the back garage door.

"Are you all right in there? Fiona, do you like your surprise?"

Breaking apart from our embrace, I want to scold Holmes for his bad timing, but then I realize it's because he doesn't want any human mating happening on his watch.

I reluctantly open the door to find Holmes and Renoir ogling the Tesla. Holmes darts inside, sniffing all around the car.

I reach into my pocket and hand Fiona the car's keycard. "The S model doesn't need keys. Just tap the card anywhere on the car or use the Tesla app."

She smiles. "I thought it would have some kind of magical way to enter the car."

I chuckle. "I did use magic to create it, but I copied the real car in every way except for the custom paint color and interior. Also, I changed your display screen to a magical one in case you need to communicate with me or the Order."

Fiona taps the keycard on the pillar next to the driver's window and the driver's door pops open.

She snuggles into the front seat like it's her favorite throw blanket. "The leather seats are the most beautiful shade of pale blue."

"I thought it worked well with the peacock blue exterior."

I can tell she wants to leap out of the car and kiss me again, but with Holmes and Renoir looking on she stays put. "I have one question for you."

"Sure, shoot."

She runs her hands over the rectangular shaped steering wheel. "How did you know my dream car was a Tesla S model?"

I give her a sheepish grin. "I might have read your mind a tiny bit."

&.

FIONA'S NEW TESLA PULLS INTO MY DRIVEWAY AND I'm glad she seems to have cooled down. She was less than thrilled last night when she realized I read her mind when I promised I wouldn't. Even the fact that I did it to gift her the car of her dreams didn't sway her.

Holmes sits at my feet. "Human women can be so difficult to understand. I thought after I saw Fiona's horrified reaction when you admitted you read her mind that she surely wouldn't talk to you for at least a week."

I pat him on the head knowing he is only trying to be supportive in his own way. "I doubt Fiona has totally forgiven me. But her gorgeous new car has obviously eased the pain."

The back door of the Tesla opens, and Holmes jumps in. The passenger door remains closed. I stand waiting to see if Fiona will back out and leave me standing in the driveway. A minute goes by and I'm about to walk into the house to get my Beemer keys when the passenger door pops open.

Fiona leans over and gives me a big smile. "Sorry. I'm still learning the ins and outs of the car."

Fiona is the type of person who would pore over the car manual like she's studying for a college entrance exam. But I ignore her remark, return her smile, and say, "It is a very high-tech car."

She backs up the Tesla and heads down the side streets she now knows well and up the on-ramp to the 405 freeway. "I want to thank you again for my amazing gift. Although I still don't approve of your method of obtaining the information on which car I wanted."

"Fair enough." I settle into the sporty leather seat, relieved I won't be let off on some street corner. "I wanted to tell you a few things about the car that aren't in the manual."

She beams. "Are there special buttons like in the Bond cars?"

Holmes barks. "Does it have a hidden jet engine under the hood?"

Another example of information Holmes has gleaned from watching TV in his downtime. "No. But I have put two key defense spells on the car. The first is activated when a possible thief approaches the car. They won't see a fancy Tesla, instead they will see a red twenty-year-old Toyota Corolla."

She chuckles. "Smart. I was wondering how I was

going to be able to keep someone from stealing the car. It's so beautiful."

I'm glad to hear she loves her gift. I truly wanted it to be the best gift she ever received. It's also an example of my magical skills.

"Don't worry. I grew up in LA. I know the risks of having a desirable car. So many times, my Beemer would have been history if not for my protection spells."

"You mentioned another level of protection. Although the first one sounds like it is all I will need."

If only that were true. "Carjacking is another big problem. The second spell causes the car to taser anyone it senses is dangerous."

Her eyes grow wide. "You mean I don't need to push a button or anything?"

I shake my head. "No. The car will know."

Renoir barks. "Your magic is truly magnifique."

I turn to face her. "Why thank you, Renoir."

Fiona comes to the exit for La Brea Boulevard. "We're getting close to Brad's apartment. He lives at Park La Brea. Do you know it?"

"It's a fixture in this part of LA. When you see it, I bet you would never guess it's seventy years old. And although I never visited her there, Avalon, Graham's now wife, lived there for a bit to evade the dark elves that were after her."

She laughs. "Dark elves? You must be jesting."

"I wish I was. The Dökkálfar were trying to take

down Los Angeles just as the vampire king Murdock tried to."

"It seems several paranormals have a passionate dislike for your hometown."

I sigh. "If only it was something as simple as dislike of a city. Unfortunately, there are evil paranormals out there that sense weakness in the leadership of Los Angeles and decided to use it as their prime location to take over humans."

Her hands nervously grip the steering wheel. "Are there any takeovers going on right now?"

Stroking her hand to calm her down, I say, "No, just the rogue shifter. The Order monitors activity every minute to make sure we stay ahead of the bad guys."

Fiona gives me a weak smile. "That's good to hear." Her hands relax and she lets out an exhale. "Guess we should get back to the business at hand. I wanted to quickly go over my strategy for the interview with Brad."

"I'm so glad you still want to work with me."

She squeezes my hand back. "Of course I do. Having a wizard of the Twelfth Order as a partner is a must if Los Angeles is as dangerous as you say."

Part of me is offended. I want Fiona to want me not because I am a wizard from a powerful Order, but for me. I plaster a smile on my face and say, "Always at your service."

With genuine warmth in her voice she says, "I know you will always look out for me. Just promise never to read my mind again." She gives me a sly smile. "And really mean it this time."

I cross my heart. "I promise."

She leans over and kisses me on the cheek. "I believe you. Now back to my strategy."

One thing I admire about Fiona is she is the consummate detective. Even when chaos looms around her she keeps her focus on her cases. "Okay, I'm all ears."

"Brad seems to be quite confused about the two weeks in question. The shifter normally would not have the magic to erase Brad's memory. It is becoming more and more obvious the shifter is not working alone. A wizard is helping him."

I nod my head. "Right. I came to the same conclusion. Hopefully Brad can give us a clue as to whom it might be."

Fiona turns the corner, and I can see the main tower of the Park La Brea apartments looming closer. "Yes, that's why I wanted to talk strategy. I want us to tag team him." She looks in the rearview mirror. "And I want to bring Holmes in as a service animal. It seems Brad has a weakness for dogs. He mentioned how guilty he felt when he forgot to walk his friend's dog as he promised."

Holmes sits up in the back seat. "Wonderful! I get to work again." He looks over at Renoir. "Fiona, can Renoir be your service dog as well?"

Renoir sits up with anticipation on her face. The poor thing hasn't been given a chance to work so far.

Fiona looks at Renoir in the rearview mirror. "I do have a plan for you, girl. Do you think you could be our sentry?"

"Sentry? What do you mean?"

I turn to face Renoir. "Fiona means you will be our look out. I assume she will tie you up outside and that you will attack anyone suspicious coming near the apartment."

"Do you mean a wizard like yourself?"

"Yes. But how will you know?"

She makes a snuffling noise like Holmes when he laughs. "Why by scent of course."

Holmes chimes in. "I never wanted to offend you, Derrick, but wizards have a slightly unpleasant odor."

This is news to me. But I try not to act offended. As long as Holmes doesn't say I smell like garbage. "Alright. Just spit it out."

Renoir responds. "You know the distinct smell of verbena?"

I shake my head but Fiona nods. "Yes, I do. But Derrick doesn't smell like verbena."

Holmes chuckles. "Of course, he doesn't to you." He eyes Renoir. "But to us you reek of it."

I try not to wince. "Okay, so canines have a dislike for how we wizards smell."

Fiona is smart enough not to ask what she as a shifter smells like. Instead, she pulls up to the main tower at Park La Brea and says, "Showtime."

While I conjure the service vest for Holmes, Fiona parks the car and pulls Renoir's leash out of the center console. She pets Renoir on the fluffy pom pom on her head. "You know what you need to do. If you see someone paranormal come close to the building, break free of your leash and attack."

"I will, mistress."

Holmes chuffs. "Poodles are not attack dogs."

Renoir huffs. "Neither are Bloodhounds."

With a stalemate reached, we pull the dogs out of the car and get to work. I cast a protection spell on Renoir. The same one I used on Holmes when we were on the death by carrots case. If anyone tries to hurt Renoir or steal her, they will get zapped with 500,000 volts of energy. I watch as Fiona finds a mid-sized palm tree and lightly ties the leash end around the trunk. It's just for show. Renoir would never runaway.

Holmes tugs on his leash. "What is my assignment?"

"If the witness Brad makes any fast moves pin him down."

Holmes barks his approval. "It is wonderful to be back in action."

He's laying on the guilt, but I smile and pat his head. "Don't worry, I can feel the case heating up. I'm going to need you with me at all times."

There is a big debate whether dogs can smile or not, but I know Holmes has a shit eating grin on his face.

Fiona joins us slightly out of breath. "Why does Holmes look so happy?"

I chuckle. "I gave him some good news. Now let's go get some of our own."

❧

FIONA RINGS THE DOORBELL OF APARTMENT 406. A brown eye looks through the old-fashioned peephole. Brad slowly opens the door but only part way. He looks at Fiona. "You didn't say anything about bringing a dog." He pauses and takes in Holmes's large body. "And a big one at that."

She graces him with one of her most charming smiles. "Oh, I'm sorry. This is my partner Mr. Dunne." She glances at the big lug sitting next to me. "This is his service dog Holmes." She leans in closer to Brad, who still hasn't opened the door all the way. "He has a case of PTSD."

Brad nods and lets us in. "I have twenty minutes to spare. I have a new job bartending at Club 88."

Brad must be good at his job. Club 88 is for the high rollers of Los Angeles. The drinking spot of the moment.

Fiona looks around the totally empty apartment living room. "Did you just move here?"

He shakes his head. "No, I've been here for a year. I live in my bedroom."

Taking in Brad's movie star good looks, I can imagine his bed gets quite the workout.

Fiona takes the comment in stride. "As you are in a

hurry, I wondered if you came up with any new information you wanted to share."

He shrugs and runs his fingers through his hair. "I told you my memory of that time is really sketchy. It's probably not anything to do with the case but I've had a recurring dream since Max died. We are joking around and he's doing magic at the bar as usual and then suddenly I'm tied up in a dark room with a gag in my mouth. A man hovers over me, but I can't see his face. His voice is a deep baritone. He says he is going to murder someone, and I will be blamed for it."

Fiona and I stare at each other, and I hop into her mind. "That isn't a dream. The shifter kidnapped Brad."

10

THE RENOIR MYSTERY

We stride out of Brad's apartment, excited to have a true suspect in the Grump case. A trip to the Order Headquarters is just what we need to track down the shifter. The Order's state of the art magical equipment should find the shifter with all the clues we have gathered.

As we stand in the courtyard in front of the impressive multicolored tower with a large circular fountain in the courtyard bubbling away, Fiona lets out a gasp. Her beautiful black standard poodle is no longer tied to the middle palm tree.

Fiona blurts out. "Renoir is missing!"

Holmes catches Renoir's scent and takes off like a shot, leaving Fiona and I to race behind him. Park La Brea is a huge complex of multiple towers and smaller housing complexes that takes up over one hundred acres. Renoir could be anywhere.

I stop running. "Fiona, it's no use. Let Holmes do what he is trained for. He will find Renoir far faster than we can."

Fiona catches her breath. "But how will you know?"

"Let's go back to the car. I can use your screen to view where Holmes is."

She nods. "Sorry, I keep forgetting you're not like my average partner."

I smile, knowing I am nothing like her ex-partner Noah, who not only was a lousy detective but an even worse boyfriend. "Yes, partnering up with a wizard does have its advantages."

Once we settle into the Tesla, I tap the screen and it quickly shows us a bird's eye view of Holmes casing each complex one by one. His black and tan body races past tall palm trees and large circular fountains surrounded with perfectly manicured flowerbeds that could rival the ones at Disneyland.

Fiona points to one of eighteen towers that make up the main Park La Brea housing complex. "How many units are there?"

"Over four thousand I believe. It is one of the biggest housing complexes ever built in the United States."

We watch Holmes as he sniffs the edge of the main swimming pool and then runs for it when a blonde woman in a black bikini screams out to the man next to her, "There's a large dog coming toward me. He looks vicious!""

We both laugh. Fiona says, "I think that woman is what you call a drama queen. Homes was at least a hundred feet away from her."

I nod. "Some people are intimidated by large dogs." I point to the screen. "Look! That's Renoir's fluffy tail sticking out from behind a hedge by that building."

Holmes sees her too and ducks behind the hedge. Fiona stabs at the screen. "Can you cast a spell so we can hear them?"

I shake my head. "My listening in spell works for humans only. But I can pop into Holmes's mind and see what's going on."

She gives me a smirk. "Seems like you enjoy popping into any creature's brain."

Judging by the tone of her voice, Fiona is a bit jealous of my skill. "I do. Did you know squids have the intelligence of a dog?"

She gives my arm a little punch. "Stop it. You're being nit."

I ignore her insult. "It's true. Although their language takes some major magic to decipher."

"How about you find out what happened to Renoir and stop telling tall tales?"

I wish I could prove to her I wasn't pulling her leg. On one of my reconnaissance missions for the Order, I gleaned vital information from a squid at an aquarium.

I pop inside Holmes's mind. "Hey, what happened to Renoir?"

Holmes lets out a mental sigh. "I was just getting

her to divulge all the juicy details and then you have to show up."

"Okay, I'll be quiet and let you listen to what she witnessed. You can fill me in on the rest of her story later."

Holmes ignores me and goes back to his conversation with Renoir. "Can you tell me what the man looked like?

"He was about medium height but stocky. He had a large posterior. I stayed far behind so he wouldn't notice me. He had the distinct smell of honeysuckle, just like Fiona. I knew he had to be up to something as he had an object projecting out of his trouser pocket. I decided I should follow him as he headed to the main parking garage. The man strolled over to an older black Mercedes, looked around, and when a couple left their car, he crawled underneath it. When the man crawled out from under the car, the object in his pocket was gone."

I practically scream out, "The shifter put a bomb under Brad's car."

Fiona's driver side door opens. "We have to stop Brad from getting to his Mercedes."

We speed toward the main tower past the big circular fountain and toward the parking garage.

As we get closer, Fiona pulls me aside. "If the shifter is working with a wizard, he could have disabled the cameras in the parking garage, couldn't he?"

Why didn't I think of that? Fiona always thinks of

every detail. "Yes. And they could have just as easily put them back on when the shifter left."

"Exactly. While you use your magic to disarm the bomb, I'm going to turn into a large cat and dislodge the device. Just keep a look out for the shifter Renoir described. If Brad shows up stall him."

It sounds like a brilliant plan except for one thing. "If I disarm the bomb, why do you need to dislodge it?"

Her eyes narrow. "Fingerprints. Shifters expend a lot of energy transforming. Sometimes we forget important details."

"Like wearing gloves."

She nods. "Exactly." Fiona moves behind one of the large clumps of palm trees that frame the entrance to the garage. In a flash, a large fluffy striped Maine Coon cat creeps out from between the palm trees and scurries into the parking garage. Fiona makes sure to keep close to the outer edge outside of the parking area. The good thing about this time of day is everyone is distracted. They want to get home and relax. So even though there are several people pulling into their assigned parking slots and getting out of their cars, no one is paying any attention to a cat lingering by a black Mercedes.

I hover by the entrance nearest Brad's car knowing that he needs to head out to his job at Club 88. Fiona disappears under his car just as I see Brad stroll into the garage dressed in his bartender uniform of a pair of tight black skinny jeans and an equally tight black long-sleeved shirt. He looks like a model *for Details*

Magazine. Brad must get a lot of tips from his eager customers. Knowing Fiona hasn't had near enough time to dislodge the bomb, I try to not act like a stalker and pretend to bump into Brad.

"Hey, don't I know you?" Then he stops and looks to my side. "Where is your dog?"

I'd totally forgotten about Holmes. Which gives me the perfect excuse. "He got scared by a loud backfire and took off. I've been looking all over the complex for him."

Brad nods sympathetically. "It must be nerve wracking for you knowing he's a service dog."

Another little detail I forgot. I clench and unclench my fists. "Yes, it is very disturbing. He's never done this to me before."

I see Fiona in cat form scurry out from under the car and duck behind one of the big round support columns.

Brad looks down at his watch and then says, "I would help you find your dog but I'm already running a bit late."

What a nice guy. I feel even worse about what the shifter has done to him. "No problem. I'm sure he'll turn up soon. It's almost dinner time."

He gives me a weak smile and then dashes off to his car. I watch as he backs up, exposing an object about the size of a pack of cigarettes resting in the parking slot. The object sits in a small puddle of oil which hopefully hasn't removed any of the fingerprints. I conjure a pair of blue plastic gloves and an evidence bag, hoping Fiona's hunch is right.

An older woman wearing a purple velvet yoga outfit voice echoes through the parking garage. "Hey, you over by the Mercedes. What are you stuffing in your pocket?" She pulls out her ancient cell phone. "You don't look like you belong here. I'm going to call the police if you don't leave immediately."

The last thing I need is for the police to show up. Mr. Kumar would not look kindly on having to rescue my butt like he did back in my early days. By the time I dodge the busy body and get well past the parking garage, I realize I need to get back to the palm trees where Fiona will surely be headed. Hiding behind a large hedge nearby I wait for a loud rustling noise. Sure enough, Fiona has transformed back to her beautiful self. Not one hair is out of place and her pantsuit is as pristine as ever. Fiona always praises my magic but hers is formidable as well.

I give her a slight bow. "Very nicely done." I hold out the evidence bag that almost blew my cover. "We need to get this to the Order lab ASAP."

She nods. "Right, as soon as the dogs return."

"No problem. I'll send it to the lab with magic."

Fiona doesn't hear me; she's too busy scanning the area for the dogs.

My brow furrows. "What the heck is keeping them? They should have returned by now."

"Hopefully no one has called the city dog catchers. Can you do a location spell to find them?"

"No. I have a better idea. I'll just pop into Holmes's mind. That will do the trick."

She laughs. "I can think of nothing more attention getting."

I don't laugh. Instead, I pop in Holmes's mind. Then I let out a gasp. "No way."

Fiona moves next to me. "What's wrong? Did the shifter return and find the dogs?"

"No, but you aren't going to be happy."

She takes my hand. "Derrick, has Renoir been injured?"

"No. But it looks like she and Holmes have consummated their relationship."

"What do you mean?"

"They have mated."

THE RIDE BACK TO WI-6 IS AN UNCOMFORTABLE ONE. Both Holmes and Renoir pretend to be sleeping in the back seat knowing full well I know what they have been up to. The nerve of Holmes. He constantly played watchdog over my love life with Fiona and the first chance he got he slept with her dog.

Fiona chats away about filling out report forms for Mr. Pierre even though Ms. Burke told Fiona he was away on a two-week holiday. That would explain the fact that all the other detectives at WI-6 headquarters are never at work.

My phone buzzes in my pocket and I dread seeing

who it is. The Order is surely monitoring my activities. If they saw the mishap in the parking garage, I will never hear the end of it. I look at the digits and recognize they are special Order numbers. "Hello?"

A slightly familiar British voice comes on the line. "I'm sorry to disturb you, mate."

It's Graham, my former bodyguard in the UK. "What's up?"

"You know that dinner I promised you back in London?"

"The one where I get the pleasure of your now wife Avalon's company."

He doesn't sound amused. "Yes, indeed. I was wondering if perhaps you are free tonight?"

There is an underlying strain in his voice that I can't ignore. Whatever Fiona had planned has to be put aside. "As a matter of fact, I am." I give Fiona a smile. "Do you mind if I bring a plus one?"

"Of course, if it is the lovely Ms. Singh."

"It is. What time and where?"

"Six o'clock at my place. Twenty-twelve Pacoima Court Studio City. You can't miss it. I bought a place that reminds me of home."

❦

FIONA STOPS IN FRONT OF THE PERFECT FACSIMILE OF an English cottage. The house has dormers on either side of a peaked front porch with ivy crawling up the porch columns and onto the front of the cream-colored house. Little sections of bricks peak out amongst the lime coated façade. "Graham wasn't kidding. The house looks like it was plucked from the British countryside and plopped down in Los Angeles."

Fiona parks in the driveway. "Truly it does." She looks back at Holmes and Renoir who are still faking being asleep. "You two have been very naughty." She glares at Holmes, and then at Renoir. "Your behavior has been a disappointment, Renoir. What do you have to say to defend yourself?"

This is going to be interesting watching Fiona interrogate her dog.

In her lovely French accent she says, "I have been very lonely and as we have not been working that much together. I spent my time at the bungalow with Holmes. At first, he repulsed me. He was so lumbering, and he drools a lot. But then his charms began to reveal themselves, along with his prowess." She looks up at Fiona with an expression of pure love. "I became enamored with him, and well, mating is a pleasant way to pass the time."

So, the tryst in the bushes wasn't the first time they were together. How ironic that my dog is getting more action than I am.

Fiona crinkles up her nose in disgust as if she is listening to her parents talk about having sex. "Don't worry. I will not make the mistake of letting you stay alone with Holmes again."

I suddenly feel the need to defend the budding

canine romance. "I think you are being a bit harsh, Fiona."

Before she can respond, I see Graham pop out of the front door of his cottage and walk down the brick pathway toward us.

He taps on the driver's side door. Fiona puts down the window and Graham leans inside. "Is everything alright?"

Fiona's cheeks blush with a hint of red. She doesn't want to explain what we were talking about.

"Everything is fine, mate. We were just discussing our dogs. Whether we should leave them in the car, or ask you if we can bring them in."

Graham looks back at Holmes. "Why, of course you can bring them inside. I'm sure Koldo would enjoy some company.

I forgot about Avalon's Shepherd familiar. "Wonderful. We'll be right in."

As Fiona watches Graham walk back down the brick path and into his house,

she gives me a weak smile. "Thank you for handling the situation. I assume Koldo is a dog."

"Yes, he's Avalon's familiar, a Basque Shepherd."

Fiona nods. "Of course. I'd forgotten you told me Avalon was a witch."

Holmes sits up looking a bit nervous. "Does Koldo do magic? Do I need you to cast a protection spell?"

What a funny thing for him to say. "I'm sure Koldo knows some magic, but as far as I know familiars only use their magic with their witches' blessing."

"That is jolly good news." He looks over at Renoir. "Don't worry, I will protect you from his advances."

I try not to gag. Holmes is laying it on thick to impress Renoir. "Stop talking, let's get inside. I'm sure Avalon has dinner ready. Keep your doggie drama to yourselves." I open the door and they jump out. Part of me wonders if I should cast a spell so they behave themselves. No. I decide to live dangerously.

Avalon greets us at the hobbit-like arched front door. She is stunning as ever with her big dark eyes and huge smile. The black jersey dress she wears fits her like a glove. It's surely one of her own creations. I heard from Krissy her clothing boutique on Melrose is a hot fashion spot.

Avalon reaches out and gives me a hug. "Derrick, it's been ages."

I give her a quick hug, mindful of Fiona looking on. "I must say marriage agrees with you."

She laughs. "You say that to all the girls."

We walk inside the entryway accented by an arched opening artfully framed by dark brown beams. The cottage has a Tudor feel inside.

Koldo comes bounding over. He has grown much taller. He nods and says in Basque accented English, "Good to see you."

Funny, I can't remember the last time I saw him. Probably at a coven meeting with the Norwegian high priestess.

The dogs shyly move behind me. "Koldo, this is

Renoir, my partner Fiona's dog and the big slobbering mass of black and tan is Holmes. He's mine."

Koldo barks and the other dogs bark back, and they head off to another part of the house.

Avalon smiles. "I told Koldo to entertain his doggy guests. I also put out two big bowls of food in case they are hungry, and a bowl of water."

"Fantastic." The distinct aroma of braised beef, onions and spices fill the air. "Whatever you have cooking in the kitchen smells marvelous."

Graham beams. "It's a Basque dish Avalon learned to cook from her grandmother."

It hits me that I have no idea if Fiona can cook. Not that it is a requirement, but it would be nice if she did, as I love Indian food. "You're a lucky man."

Avalon excuses herself and Graham leads us past an impressive main room with a heavy beamed vaulted ceiling into another room that has an arched opening. The dining room table is set for four and has a long platter in the middle scattered with a few appetizers.

Graham motions for us to sit on either side of the table. "Please help yourselves to a few appetizers. Avalon should be out in a moment."

My stomach grumbles and I grab a cracker topped with a wedge of cheese and a slice of bacon off the center platter and put them on a small plate. "I'm looking forward to a wonderful meal, but I know that is not the reason we are here."

Fiona eyes me as she places a few of the appetizers on her plate as well. I'm certain she would rather have a pleasant meal and get to know my friends than find out the real reason we are at their home later. But that isn't my style. I won't possibly be able to enjoy the wonderful Basque meal Avalon has prepared while I'm sitting nervously trying to figure out why Graham reached out to me.

Graham flinches. "I should know you would want to pry the reason out of me before we eat dinner."

"You know how impatient I can be."

He nods. "Then I will rip off the Band-Aid, so to speak. I know you are trying to track down a shifter that is causing problems with wizards. Well, I am afraid we have been one of the shifter's targets. If it wasn't for my bodyguard training and the fact I know Avalon like the back of my hand, we wouldn't be having this dinner this evening. We'd be meeting at Avalon's funeral."

The pain on Graham's face is real. Mine would be too if someone tried to kill Fiona. "I'm so sorry. I hate to put on my detective hat, but can you tell me exactly what happened?"

Avalon comes out of the kitchen carrying a large platter with a rack of lamb. "Here's the main course. Graham, can you help me with the sides?"

Being the dutiful husband, Graham flies out of his chair and disappears into the kitchen. Fiona leans toward me and whispers, "It's the shifter; it has to be. Didn't Mr. Kumar put you back on Zoomer duty for this very reason?"

I nod my head. "Yes. But how can one shifter cause trouble for so many people?"

Fiona's eyes narrow. "I've been pondering the same thing and I think I have an explanation that doesn't involve another shifter."

Unfortunately, her huge revelation will have to wait as Avalon and Graham return carrying a large bowl of roasted potatoes and a small platter with asparagus covered with tiny slivers of bacon.

I beam at Avalon. "Everything smells delicious."

Graham sits down at the head of the table and Avalon follows suit. Any conversation about the shifter will have to wait until after dinner. Not only do I not want to be rude, but my stomach is doing flip flops as the aromas of roasted lamb and potatoes mingle with the asparagus. As Graham carves up the lamb roast, Avalon hands the potatoes to Fiona. How does a compelling conversation about the evils of the paranormal world turn into one about food? Between bites of lamb and potatoes, Fiona asks Avalon questions about her family, who the recipes are from. Graham and I prove we are typical men whose worlds are ruled by their stomachs.

When we are stuffed and can't eat any more, Avalon pops up from her chair. "Who wants a slice of lemon tart and a cup of tea?"

Fiona loosens her pants waistband. "It sounds lovely, but can we have a bit of a respite first?"

Avalon smiles. "You sound like Graham. He swears he's put on ten pounds since we've been married."

I glance over at Graham, who on the surface looks the same but then I notice his strong jawline is not quite as pronounced and there is a slight bulge creeping over his jeans' waistline. He rubs his little tummy. "It's true. I'd be even bigger if I didn't cast the occasional slimming spell."

Avalon's eyes twinkle. "I admit I have to do the same or I would never fit in the clothes I design."

Fiona looks at Avalon with a bit of envy in her eyes. "I wish I could do the same. Ever since I hit my late twenties, I have to be more aware of what I eat."

I lean back in my chair unable to keep the chit chat going. I look straight into Avalon's eyes. "I know I'm asking a lot for you to relive what happened with the shifter, but Fiona and I really would like to stop him from doing any more damage. He almost took your life, and he did take Mr. Grump's."

Graham shifts in his chair, "Not the Grump of the magic act Grump and Son?"

I sigh. "Yes. Maxwell Grump, the father."

Graham balls his fists. "I used to watch their act whenever I could get a chance. Their magic was seamless. Almost as if they were wizards."

I nod. "I never saw Maxwell perform in person, but I did see Buddy, the son, perform the bottle trick."

Fiona leaned forward in her chair as if Buddy had suddenly materialized in the dining room and was going to perform the bottle trick all over again. "We sat right next to him the whole time he did the trick. The way he kept placing nails into a bottle filled with water while holding it upside down took my breath away."

Avalon joined in. "They were both so talented. Why would the shifter want to kill Mr. Grump?"

I bit my lip wishing I had the answer. "That is what Fiona and I are trying to find out."

❧

I LOOK OVER AT FIONA, FEELING COMPLETELY drained. "What a day. All I want to do is crawl into bed and sleep for ten hours."

She pulls into my driveway and puts the car in park. "I'm with you." She turns toward the backseat where the dogs are sleeping soundly. Holmes is doing his usual slobbery snore. "They are exhausted too."

I give Fiona a wink. "It's been a big day for all of us."

I wish Fiona didn't live so close as it would be nice to have her in my bed tonight. Not to do anything sexual like Holmes and Renoir, but to have a familiar warm body spoon me to sleep.

Fiona looks at me and yawns. "Do you mind if we spend the night with you? I'm exhausted."

For once I feel like Fiona read my mind. "No trouble." I snap my fingers. "The bed has clean sheets and is ready for us."

"You're right." She gives me a tired smile. "Having a wizard partner has many advantages."

We are about to exit the car when a call comes through the screen. The number looks familiar, but I can't place it.

Fiona pushes the answer button. "Hello, this is Ms. Singh."

"I'm sorry to disturb you so late in the evening, but the result of the final lab test came in on Maxwell Grump, and I thought you should know right away."

I would have bet the day couldn't get any more eventful and I would have lost.

Fiona perks up. "That's wonderful news. How exactly did Mr. Grump die? Was it truly from the over consumption of beer?"

The coroner's voice remains steady. "Not exactly. It wasn't the alcohol in the beer that did him in, but the yeast."

Fiona and I look at each other both thinking the same thing. I turn to her and say, "So your original second choice of death turns out to be correct. The yeast built up in his body and killed him."

"Yes, that is what happened, but it was not because of the normal level of yeast in beer. Usually there is between 0.007 to 0.015 in a darker beer. But Mr. Grump's blood test came back at 1.05. More than enough to kill him. Which leads me to assume someone added the extra yeast to the beer when he was quite drunk, so he didn't notice the bitter flavor. Similar to..."

I cut in. "Similar to the death by carrots case."

The coroner taps on something, then says, "Yes. Mr. Grump definitely died from yeast intoxication not a heart attack. That high of an amount of yeast causes a chain reaction in the body. All his major internal organs shut down."

My heart aches for Mr. Grump. It had to be a very painful death. "This time it's not a waitress spiking smoothies with toxic levels of vitamin A like the death by carrots case. It's a bartender spiking beers with yeast."

The coroner lets out a sigh. "I'm afraid so. It's murder for certain."

11

SO CLOSE

As tough as yesterday was, I have a feeling today is going to go much better. My dream came true last night. Fiona spooned me as we slept.

I kiss her cheek and her eyes flutter open. She looks around my bedroom, trying to orient herself. Then she runs her hands down her pantsuit clad body. "All I remember was stumbling through the front door."

I pull a few long strands of her hair off her face. "I didn't need to cast a sleeping spell last night. We were both exhausted."

She runs her hand along my bare chest. "At least you had the energy to take your shirt off."

"It's one of my favorite shirts." I chuckle. "Figured you would keep me warm."

She runs her fingers along my biceps. "One day I will be able to explore your muscles further."

I so want her to do it now but a howling sound

from the other side of my door. "I'm starving. Wake up!"

It figures Holmes would continue to foil my romance with Fiona when he already has one with Renoir.

Fiona gets up from the bed. "I should go home and change. "She looks down at her pants suit, which is quite wrinkled. "I am a mess."

I give her a smile. "A lovely mess. You know I can conjure up whatever outfit you would like."

Fiona bends down and strokes my face. "I appreciate the offer, but I should get Renoir home. She needs a break from your randy dog."

"I'd take offense, but it's true. I'll meet you at the office. Something tells me Mr. Pierre is back."

Fiona nods. "I feel his presence in my bones. He wasn't on a vacation, he was surely plotting something. We should see Mr. Bullock first."

"You're right. I'm sure our occasional reports haven't made him very happy."

Fiona opens the bedroom door. "His hands-off approach with this case has been remarkable."

And somewhat alarming, I think to myself. We've been so busy I never questioned not hearing from Mr. Bullock or his assistant Scott. The little hairs on the back of my neck prickle. A force is slowly building like a hurricane off in the ocean and I need to up my game. "You're right. More reason to meet with Mr. Bullock ASAP."

As I watch Fiona leave, Holmes tosses his muzzle in my lap. "I thought she would never go home."

I bop his nose. "That's not nice, Holmes. I'm certain Renoir will be grateful for a break though."

His eyes narrow. "I see. This is your revenge for my mating multiple times with Renoir."

He would have to rub it in. "I think you should reconsider your choice of words."

Holmes makes a snarling noise. "Why?"

My canine sidekick sure is pushing his luck. "Because I control your food and I may decide you need to go on a long term fast."

IT'S BEEN FOREVER SINCE FIONA AND I STOOD IN MR. Bullock's office. The leather executive chair behind his large walnut desk sits empty. A feeling of unbalanced energy fills the room.

Scott's smiling face eases my apprehension a tiny bit. "It's so good to see you two."

I eye the generous number of muffins and fruit laid out on the console table as well as a large carafe of coffee. Holmes follows my gaze hoping for a handout. "Thanks so much for the wonderful food selections. I didn't have a chance to grab any breakfast."

He beams. "I know."

Did he read my mind when I first walked in the office? Probably. Fiona walks over to one of the parson chairs in front of the walnut desk. "I had a protein shake but thank you, Scott."

"I knew you were fine." He straightens his lavender tie. "The food is for the ever absent minded Mr. Dunne."

He says it with affection in his voice, so I don't take offense. Instead, I get up and head straight for the console table. I load down a square plate with two muffins and cut up fruit. When I return to my chair, a small table has conveniently materialized next to it. A huge mug of coffee with a splash of cream just the way I like it rests on the corner of the table.

Fiona pets Renoir sitting dutifully by her side, then eyes the empty desk and says to Scott, "Do you know when Mr. Bullock will be arriving?"

"He had an important meeting, but he promised he would leave it early. He's been wanting to catch up with the Unusual Death Squad."

Fiona chuckles. "I forgot about the brilliant name Mr. Bullock bestowed on us."

My curiosity gets the better of me and I hope I don't breach any WI-6 etiquette by my question. "I have been surprised Mr. Bullock has been so hands off on our case."

Scott runs his fingers through his immaculately styled hair. "There has been a lot going on. I believe I spoke with you about the problem before."

Interesting. Scott doesn't feel comfortable enough to speak freely. The war between Mr. Pierre and Mr. Bullock must have really heated up."

I nod. "I understand."

Fiona's brow furrows but she says nothing. She can sense the building tension in the room. Fiona is smart enough to put two and two together and know what has kept Mr. Bullock preoccupied, his nemesis—Mr. Pierre.

I take the opportunity to inhale the blueberry muffins and fruit while we wait. The temperature in the office drops a few degrees as a fine pale lavender mist fills the room. Mr. Bullock appears in his chair looking worse for wear. He has dark circles under his eyes and his usually tanned skin is decidedly pale. But the thing that truly makes me uneasy is the fact that his pride and joy mustache is gone.

Fiona sits nervously biting her lip and staring at the blank space above Mr. Bullock's upper lip.

Mr. Bullock forces a smile. "It's so nice to have the Unusual Death Squad in my office again. It has been a while." He touches his upper lip. "Yes, my mustache is gone. It was not of my doing. But I decided it was time for a change."

The hairs on my neck prickle again. "Not of my doing" echoes in my ears.

Fiona leans a bit forward. "I must say you look handsome either way."

My partner, ever the peacemaker and diplomat.

Mr. Bullock gives her a weak smile. "It has taken a bit of getting used to. I've had the mustache for over a decade."

I can't stand the suspense of not knowing what

happened to the missing mustache any longer. My answers can only be achieved one way. I pop into Scott's mind. "Did Mr. Pierre take away Mr. Bullock's mustache?"

Scott doesn't hesitate. "I was hoping you would enter my mind. I have been unable to inform you about what has been going on. It's been complete chaos here at WI-6 headquarters. They have been conjuring away each other's mustaches for the last two weeks. I wish I could say that is all they have done to each other."

That explains why Mr. Bullock looks so pale. I can't wait to see what Mr. Pierre looks like. I'm team Bullock all the way. "I'm so sorry to hear the war has spiraled out of control."

Scott lets out a deep exhale. "You have no idea. This problem with the shifter has only made things worse."

"The rogue shifter is Mr. Pierre's doing, isn't it?"

Mr. Bullock glares at Scott. "Can we please keep to the business at hand?"

Crap. I'm busted. Scott wrings his hands like a dishcloth. "Yes, of course, sir."

Poor Fiona looks at the three of us having no idea what is going on. Unfortunately, I can't tell her here.

Mr. Bullock looks at Fiona. "Can you please get me up to speed on the Mr. Grump case? I have not had the time to read your last report."

It's good to know Fiona has been holding up her end of the partnership by sending updates to Mr. Bullock.

"Things have changed since my last report. We can officially declare that Mr. Grumps death was murder. He was killed by an over exposure to yeast administered by the rogue shifter. He managed to implement his evil plan by posing as the bartender at Mr. Grump's favorite bar."

He rubs his chin no longer able to rub his mustache when he is deep in thought. "I'm not surprised. My gut told me that despite Mr. Grump's drinking history, the heart attack was not the cause."

Fiona nods. "Yes. The coroner confirmed the fact after the final lab results came in."

He turns to me. "I know you figured out the source of the problem."

Fiona's brow furrows, then they straighten. She has figured out that I had a private conversation with Scott in his mind.

"Yes, sir. We are so close to closing the case. We just need one final piece of the puzzle." I smile at Fiona. "And I know who has the piece."

Mr. Bullock nods. "Then go and get it."

FIONA STANDS NEXT TO ME AS WE WAIT FOR THE elevator, more confused than ever. She nervously strokes Renoir's fluffy head. "You pushed the button to *The Pit*. We aren't going to the parking garage. I thought you were in hot pursuit of..."

I put my hand up to my lips. She has a flash of

recognition that Mr. Pierre's eyes and ears are everywhere. "No. We have to check in with the team and Mr. Pierre."

We step into the elevator with the dogs pulling up the rear. Fiona eyes the corner where the camera is aimed right at us. I know she wants me to pop into her mind and fill her in, but I'm certain Mr. Pierre has a magic monitor in the elevator, so all I do is shrug. The elevator door opens and the familiar gloom of the darkly lit entrance to *The Pit*.

Holmes pauses by the door. "Something is wrong. The scent of *The Pit* is off. There is an underlying hint of decay. Not to mention a total lack of the familiar fragrance of Mr. Pierre's mustache wax."

I pat him on the head. "You will soon discover the reason it is missing."

Holmes's nose crinkles. "There is also the scent of something new—fear."

I swallow hard as Fiona and I walk into *The Pit*, ready for anything, but not what we are faced with. The office is not hidden under a cloak of darkness but is brightly lit. In fact, I could use a pair of sunglasses, it's so bright. The other obvious difference is the fact that all the desks are gone. *The Pit* is a big open space with no signs of any other detectives. Only Ms. Burke greets us. "As you can see, we are moving our offices. Our new offices will be on the twentieth floor."

Fiona looks around confused. "Should we report there?"

Ms. Burke shakes her head. "No, Mr. Pierre will see you in his usual office."

Interesting. It seems the war may have changed some of the detective's allegiances. That would be welcome news. But knowing that the place is still bugged to the hilt, I say nothing.

Ms. Burke motions toward the back of the main room and the door to Mr. Pierre's office. "He will see you now."

Fiona strides forward as if she is headed toward the gallows and is not afraid of the executioner. "Come on; might as well see what he wants."

I catch up with her and open the door. Mr. Pierre is sitting behind his desk with only the top of his shoulders and head showing as usual. But one thing has changed—his mustache.

He catches my gaze. "How kind of you to report in finally. I hope you have solved the Grump case as it may be your last."

Fiona strides up to the desk and towers over Mr. Pierre. "Must I remind you Mr. Bullock is our superior? He determines our fate."

Mr. Pierre looks up at Fiona with the twinkle of victory in his eyes. To emphasize his point, he strokes the full mustache that used to be on Mr. Bullock's face. At that moment I promise myself I will take him out —permanently.

His gaze shifts to me. "Your time in *The Pit* is numbered as well, Monsieur Dunne. New leadership is but around the corner."

I give him my best celebrity smile. I think you are mistaken, sir. You've forgotten the golden rule. Revenge proves its own executioner."

§&

MY CONFRONTATION WITH MR. PIERRE MAKES ME more determined than ever to catch the shifter. I need to convince the shifter if he doesn't come under the protection of the Order, his days are numbered. Mr. Pierre will never let the shifter live once he has outlived his usefulness.

Fiona touches my hand pulling me back to the here and now. "Are you certain Buddy is the key?"

I nod. "Yes. I realized inside his mind is the real identity of the rogue shifter."

She pulls onto the 405 freeway, and we head toward Koreatown and Buddy's apartment. "I hope you are right. The thought that not only one of my kind has killed an innocent person like Mr. Grump, but that he is actively trying to kill the loved ones of wizards of the Twelfth Order, like Avalon, makes my blood boil. We shifters have a hard enough time fitting into the paranormal world without one of us going rogue and ruining our reputations."

I can understand her anger. Shifters tend to be solitary and fly under the paranormal radar. They are very different from their werewolf cousins. I say to Fiona, "It's almost like the rogue shifter has rabies or something."

She pats me on the back. "Brilliant. That's it precisely."

Buddy opens the hobbit-like door to his 40's cottage and I barely recognize him. His face is covered by a thick mountain man beard. His T-shirt and jeans are covered in stains. The living room is scattered with take-out cartons and pizza boxes and has the distinct aroma of food on the edge of rotting. His grief for his father has taken over his life. I clench my fist knowing Mr. Pierre is the probable cause of it all. I give him a smile like he's not a total mess. "Hi, Buddy. Good to see you."

He gives me a weak smile and looks over at Fiona. "Sorry my living room looks like a frat house."

She shakes her head. "It's not a problem at all. You have a chat with Mr. Dunne, and I'll tidy up a bit."

Buddy looks horrified. "No. Please don't bother. I'm going to have my housekeeper come next week."

Fiona gives him a knowing smile. "Then at least let me clear up a few things so we can sit down."

He shrugs as Fiona marches to the kitchen and returns with a large black trash bag. In mere minutes the pizza boxes covering the couch are gone and so are the takeout boxes scattered all over the floor. She seals up the trash bag and tucks it back in the kitchen. Fiona dusts off her hands and sits down on the couch. "There." I ignore the lingering tomato sauce and sit down. "Buddy, I have a few questions for you. We are very close to solving you father's case."

His eyes grow wide. "Was it murder?"

I nod. "Yes, it appears so."

His fists ball up. "I knew it! What is his name? Is he in custody?"

I shake my head. "Not yet. We need a bit more proof. That's why I'm here. I know you mentioned seeing Mrs. Pearson, the woman in the front row, quite a few times. We did investigate her, and she has been cleared of any wrongdoing.

Buddy shifts in his chair. "I never think of women as killers, but something about Rene made me wonder."

"After speaking with her, I can understand why. She has a strong personality. Can you think back to someone else you might have noticed in the back of the theater that attended the show more than once or twice?"

He closes his eyes. I so want to pop into his mind, but Buddy is already a hot mess.

Buddy's eyes pop open and he fidgets in the club chair. "Until you asked me to harken back, I'd forgotten all about him. The man was easy to forget. Medium build, mousy brown hair, a slightly chubby nondescript face. As I recall, he came to about four or five of our shows. Always sat in the middle of the fourth row. He never approached us, so I forgot all about him."

Magicians have an amazing eye for detail and Buddy's has paid off. "Anything else you noticed that was distinguishing about him?"

He closed his eyes again. "Yes. One night I happened to see him get up and leave. Despite how ordinary he looked from the front from behind he had quite a pronounced buttock."

Fiona and I look at each other and try not to laugh then she abruptly stands up. "That is a wonderful description. We should be able to find him now."

Buddy's eyes narrow. "You think that man is the killer?"

The last thing we want is for Buddy to go out and try to track him down. I shake my head. "No, the killer would never expose himself to his victim. But there is a good chance the man worked for the killer."

Buddy's shoulders slump. "You will keep me updated, won't you?"

Fiona reaches over and squeezes Buddy's arm. "I promise."

We leave Buddy's apartment hoping we can put all the pieces together and figure out where the shifter is hiding. At least we now have a description of what he truly looks like. The Twelfth Order should find him quickly now. I text the info to Mr. Kumar on the Order direct line as we walk to the Tesla.

Fiona taps her keycard on the side of the S model and the engine roars to life. "We're so close I can feel it."

I open the passenger side door. "My wizard senses are sizzling."

Fiona slides behind the wheel and puts the car in reverse. "Can you really physically feel something is going to happen?"

"Yes, I can. Witches can too. It's more than a hunch or instinct. I know we are close to solving the case."

Fiona turns the steering wheel hard to the left. "Should we drive to Order Headquarters to see how the hunt is going?"

"Might as well, although I'm sure they will find the shifter soon."

Fiona nods and pulls out onto La Brea Boulevard. The light changes before she can make it through the intersection. "Bloody hell."

Cars aim at us like arrows from both sides of the intersection. "We can't stay here. Just gun it."

Fiona hits the accelerator just as a large semi-truck blast through the intersection. It hits the Tesla with such force we spin around and end up on the other side of the street. We are hit with such force the air bags release and both of us are covered in powder.

Fiona touches her forehead. "I'm bleeding."

I can taste blood in my mouth. I must have bit my lip when the airbag deployed. I force the airbag off my face and can see that the car is filling up with smoke. Trying to get closer to Fiona to see if she needs help, a shooting pain goes up my leg. It's pinned between the seat and the passenger door which is practically in my lap. The pain throbs again and I fight for consciousness so I can cast a healing spell for Fiona, but it is too late. My world goes blank.

12

———

THE EXECUTIONER

My eyes flicker open, and I am not inside Fiona's Tesla or in the hospital. I look around for any signs of Fiona, but there isn't even the lingering fragrance of her Shalimar perfume in the air. Was the crash a dream? If it wasn't, I'm glad we decided not to bring the dogs to Buddy's apartment. They surely would not have made it through the accident.

Eshe appears through an unfamiliar doorway. "Oh good, you are up."

I prop myself up on my elbows in a frilly pink confection of a bed. So not what I imagined Eshe would pick to be sleeping in. "What happened?"

She sits down on the edge of the bed. "Remember when the coven cast a protection spell on you and Fiona?"

"Yes."

"Built into the spell was an alarm. When the spell is triggered, every member of the coven receives a signal. I notified Mr. Kumar immediately. The Order transported you two here. Fiona's car is fully repaired and sitting in my driveway as if nothing ever happened. Would you like to see what it looked like after the semi hit you?"

My wizard senses sizzle, warning me that saying yes is not going to be pleasant, but I say it anyway. "Yes."

Eshe pulls out her cell phone and shows me a photo of the crash before it was erased from existence by the Order. I bite my lip when I see that the car, despite all its best protections, is a crumpled mess. I have no doubt in my mind if it wasn't for Eshe and my protection spell, Fiona and I at best would be severely injured or at worst, dead. "I'm grateful for the coven's work."

Eshe smiles. "I think it was a trifecta. Your spell on Fiona's car, our spell to protect you both, and the Order's amazing healing spells."

"You're right, it was a group effort."

Eshe's brow furrows. "That doesn't negate the fact that someone wanted the both of you dead."

I give her a weak smile. "We know who it is. His time will come."

She nods and holds out her hand to help me out of bed. The Order's healing spell has worked its magic. I feel almost like myself. Sitting up in bed, I slide my legs over the edge and fight back a laugh when I see Eshe has me dressed in one of her gold caftans.

Brooklyn strides into the room, takes one look at

me, and laughs. I can't help but notice she is wearing one of her black jersey body hugging outfits. Good thing I have always thought of her as my little sister. "You look like you are ready to go bar hopping with the coven."

She laughs. "No, I was supposed to have dinner with Jerome."

"Are you guys still hot and heavy?"

She gives me a devilish smile. "Yep. How can I resist a hot man who happens to be a werewolf?"

Eshe beams. "I hope one day he will become a son-in-law."

Brooklyn makes a tisk tisk sound. "Mom, you know we are taking it slow. We're too young to get married."

I try to remember exactly how old Brooklyn must be by now—twenty-four. "Sorry, Eshe. I'm with Brooklyn."

She walks over and gives me a gentle punch in the bicep. "Thanks, bro. Hey, enough talk about me. I came to tell you Fiona is resting quietly. I gave her a sleeping potion to calm her down. She feels responsible for the accident."

Just like Fiona to think that because she was behind the wheel she is to blame. "Thank you. It's been a crazy few weeks. I'm sure she could use a good night's sleep."

"No problem. She can stay in my bed for tonight. I'll head over to Jerome's. Glad you survived another close call."

"Me too."

Eshe helps me stand up. "Mr. Kumar made me

promise as soon as you were feeling better to let him know. Do you think you can withstand the transportation beam?"

If she only knew how many times I have been injured and transported before. I look down at the caftan. "My attire is not going to be received well at the Order."

Eshe giggles like a schoolgirl. "I thought it would cheer you up, but I see your point."

She mumbles a spell, and the caftan vanishes. In its place I'm wearing black jeans and a long sleeve black shirt. "Hey, why am I dressed all in black? I hope you don't think I'm headed to my own funeral."

Her eyes grow wide then she gives me a grin. "Black is also a powerful color and quite appropriate for the occasion. You are heading off to war, after all."

My eyes flicker open as the transportation beam fades away. I'm standing in front of the giant main viewing screen at Twelfth Order Headquarters, looking up at the face of my current nemesis. His chubby cheeks fill the large display screen. Just like in the movies, under his image is a caption that says in bold block letters MOST WANTED.

Holmes takes one look at his face and says, "What an unfortunate looking man. No wonder he shifts into other people."

Patting him on the head, I say, "Excellent observation, Holmes."

A hint of perfume drifts past my nose. I turn, surprised to find Fiona standing next to Mr. Kumar. She looks wide-awake. Eshe must have known Mr. Kumar's plans and cast a spell to reverse Brooklyn's sleeping potion. Fiona looks stunning as usual. Eshe dressed her in a form fitting white pants suit and high heeled matching boots. Renoir sits dutifully next to her feet scanning the room as if one of the wizards is going to attack her mistress. Not that I blame her. My gut is still churning at the thought I could have lost her.

Mr. Kumar glances over at Fiona with a look of sheer admiration. "If it wasn't for your finesse in handling Buddy Grump in his delicate condition of grief, the Order wouldn't be minutes away from locating the rogue shifter."

Fiona doesn't bask in the complement. "I give all the credit to Buddy Grump himself. Even in his state of emotional pain, his incredible memory gave us a wonderful description of the shifter. I wish all my witnesses had Buddy's eye for detail."

Mr. Kumar nods. "Yes, we are ever indebted to him. Mr. Bullock is relieved, as you can imagine."

The war for control of the WI-6 Los Angeles division will hopefully be over soon. "I had no idea when I accepted the job at WI-6 I was walking into a battle of the bosses. Something to rival Obi-Wan Kenobi and Darth Vader."

Despite my joke, Mr. Kumar stands expressionless.

In fact, he is avoiding eye contact with me. Something tickles at the back of my mind and suddenly I feel like a total idiot. My getting the job at WI-6 wasn't encouraged by the Twelfth Order; it was created by the Order. It had nothing to do with my graduating from Zoomer duty at all.

"You are wrong, Derrick. Only you could have taken on such a challenge and succeeded."

The silky-smooth voice of Mr. Kumar inside my mind does nothing for my mood. "I'll take your word for it."

Fiona reaches over and touches my hand. "Are you alright, Derrick? There is a scary blank expression on your face." Then she looks over at Mr. Kumar, staring up at the image of the shifter, and knows he is inside my mind.

There is a commotion by the control console, and I soon see why. The Exemplary Wizard himself has arrived on the scene. He is dressed in his usual Saville Row black suit and his brown hair is styled perfectly. I still smile every time I see him because I never know what form he will take. The modern wizard who stands before me now, or a traditional wizard with the flowing robes but lacking the long white beard. He quickly glances at Fiona then his eyes lock in on mine. "Mr. Dunne. It has been a while since I've had the pleasure of your company. I want to assure you that the assumption you made earlier is not a correct one."

Crap. Once again, he has read my mind. I should be used to it by now, but he is so slick about the way he does it, I'm still surprised. I can sense when Mr. Kumar hops into my mind and then out again, but the Exemplary Wizard leaves no trace. "Thank you for the reassurance, sir."

Fiona tries to catch my gaze, even more confused than ever. How can she know what is going on when there is another layer of conversation happening in our minds? I give her my best *I'll explain everything later,* smile. She nods, but I know the whole experience must be beyond frustrating. I know it was for me when I first started at the Twelfth Order. But you soon learn you will always be playing catch up when there is another conversation going on out of your reach.

The Exemplary Wizard makes a grand gesture toward the screen. "We have located the shifter but his exact location inside his home is being hidden by powerful magic." He turns to me. "It is your mission to use your dog and your reconnaissance skills to pin down his exact location."

Holmes excitedly heels next to me. I pat him on the head. "Are you ready to take out the shifter?"

He barks his approval. "Ready."

Mr. Kumar crouches down to Holmes's eye level. "The Order is counting on your acute sensory skills, Holmes."

He gives Mr. Kumar a toothy grin. "I will do you proud, sir."

Fiona and Renoir watch as the light beam pierces the ceiling of the main headquarters tunnel. Despite the Exemplary Wizard's presence, she throws me an air kiss. "Be safe."

Holmes does an involuntary yelp when he lands on the floor of the shifter's apartment after his body has completely reformed. He looks up at me, his big brown eyes full of shame. "I forgot what an out of body experience the transportation beam can be, I'm sorry if I blew our cover."

I shake my head. "Don't worry, the Order had us enter inside a sound barrier just for that reason. We don't have much time. You search the perimeter of the living room while I conjure a magic sensor."

As Holmes gets to work sniffing every surface for the distinctive sent of honeysuckle, the shifter's trademark, while I survey our surroundings.

One thing I can say about the rogue shifter, despite his ordinary looks, apart from his large butt, his home looks like it belongs on the cover of an interior decorating magazine. As much as I can't stand Mr. Pierre, I have to say when he likes someone, he does treat them well. The home's exquisite and expensive modern décor is beyond impressive. The marble floor gleams while the designer leather chairs, and sectional sofa appear to be floating several inches above the floor. That's one way to keep from scratching the stone. Of course, what the shifter doesn't know is that this beautiful home isn't a gift for him to enjoy indefinitely. The clock is ticking on his usefulness to Mr. Pierre. When the time runs out everything in the mini mansion will cease to exist along with its owner. It's amazing how naive even paranormals can be when they are showered with praise and a huge upgrade in their lifestyle.

Holmes sniffs the perimeter of the living room and motions me with his front paw when his nose hits a spot along the back wall where the giant TV and media console are located. I quickly cross the room and stand next to him.

In a low whisper he says, "Something smells out of the ordinary here. The air escaping from the crack smells totally different than the air in the rest of the house." The hair along his backbone bristles. "Something otherworldly."

I tap the earpiece Mr. Kumar gave me. "I'm going to send you some data to analyze. Holmes is sensing an extremely high level of magic here."

Taking the high-powered magic sensor I conjured, I run it along the crack. It glows purple indicating powerful magic is indeed on the other side of the wall.

I pat Holmes on the head and whisper, "You stand guard here. I'm going to have the Order transport me inside."

Worried the protective sound barrier is slowly thinning, I don't risk using the earpiece again. Instead, I reach out to Mr. Kumar. Thankfully he has left his mind open for me to enter. "Sir, it seems Mr. Pierre has created a separate space inside the home. That is where their true operations are located."

Mr. Kumar says, "Excellent work. We have scanned the hidden space and as luck would have it, Mr. Pierre is in residence."

My heart beats faster. "Get me in there right now before he leaves."

There is an uneasy pause before Mr. Kumar speaks. "I do not think that would be wise. Although your wizard skills are progressing nicely, you are not an even match for Mr. Pierre. I was going to step in at this point."

Although I warned Mr. Pierre that revenge is its own executioner, a famous quote by Henry Ford, I feel it is my obligation to seek revenge for all the people he killed. Besides, I know just what I want to do to him. "Sir, I feel a tremendous responsibility to take him out myself. He killed three people because of my involvement in WI-6. You can oversee everything that transpires and if I fail, please step in and finish him off."

Again, I am met with a moment of silence. "The Exemplary Wizard wants this issue resolved once and for all. Please don't make me regret this decision."

The pressure is on. "I won't, sir."

"I will have you transported into the hidden space but as the shifter. At the exact moment we transport you, the shifter will be beamed to headquarters."

It's a brilliant plan. One I wished I had thought of myself. "It is pure genius, sir. Thank you for the opportunity. I will not let you down."

I leave Mr. Kumar's mind and return to Holmes's. "If something goes wrong and I don't return, I'm certain Fiona will adopt you. The bonus is you get to be around Renoir all the time."

Holmes doesn't snicker. "Derrick, you must return.

The thought of living with two females is too much for me."

I chuckle. Typical of Holmes to make a joke during a serious situation. "I hope that horrible fate doesn't befall you."

Patting Homes for what could be the last time, the transportation beam descends from the ceiling, and I am gone. When my body, returns it is not my own. It doesn't take seeing myself in a mirror to tell I have acquired the identity of the shifter. My butt feels gigantic. The strain on my pants is incredibly distracting. Although my new body feels real, wizards can't actually body shift. We can only imitate the likeness of someone. Not literally become them.

The house within the mini mansion is the opposite of the one where the shifter lives. The living room is completely empty except for two folding chairs. I walk over to the bedroom to see if Mr. Pierre is inside, but he is not there. The bedroom is equally spare. It only has an old-fashioned iron bed which has chain and leather restraints anchored under the ball finals. This must have been where the shifter held Brad. Yet another person I need to seek revenge for.

I walk past another door and hear a rustling sound, and then the distinct sound of a loud fart. I stuff back a laugh, realizing I have caught Mr. Pierre in the restroom. What a wonderful compromising position I find him in.

Several different scenarios run through my mind about how to seek my revenge. Even a wizard as powerful as Mr. Pierre is at his most vulnerable when he is relieving himself. When I first was recruited for the Order, I thought they would have some amazing spell that would get rid of the need to use the bathroom. But there is no magic powerful enough to stop such a natural process in wizards. Although Mr. Bullock managed to develop a spell for dogs.

Mr. Kumar pops into my mind. "Derrick, this is no time to contemplate the failings of wizard magic. Mr. Pierre is only going to be in this delicate position for a few moments longer."

"Right. I apologize, sir." That was the kick in my newly acquired big butt I needed to stop my nerves from getting the better of me. Time to do the job I was sent here for. Taking a deep breath, I fling open the door knowing exactly what I must do. "Sir, I am so sorry to interrupt you, but I think the mansion has been compromised."

His eyes drift up from whatever he is reading on his phone, and he glares up at me. "If I still didn't need your services, I would vaporize you on the spot." Mr. Pierre flicks one side of his pencil thin mustache. "It must be an error. I have received no notification of any breach of the system."

I wish I could gloat about the fact that once again the Twelfth Order's magic is superior to other wizard's magic.

Mr. Pierre glowers at me. "Can I have some privacy? I sense no danger." To make his point he hurls a large spark at me. Mr. Pierre really must be constipated, or he would have done something far worse than send a tiny energy ball my way.

As I start to shut the door, I can hear Mr. Pierre go back to scrolling on his phone. The light tapping on glass continues and he doesn't realize that things are about to change.

Now is my moment.

Using every ounce of magic I have within me, my plan of revenge literally rains down on Mr. Pierre. First, I conjure a tsunami of beer that floods the bathroom in less than a second, next I zap his body with the same amount of vitamin A that killed Mr. Hamlyn. Flashes of energy erupt from behind the door, but I can still hear the beer flooding the room. My last revenge I must do face-to-face. Snapping my fingers, the beer vanishes as I open the bathroom door.

Mr. Pierre looks like the soaked French rat of a wizard he is. Sparks of energy bounce off the walls but don't hit me. He curses in French. "Mered!" Then he says in English, "You think you are clever, Mr. Dunne. First you pose as my puppet and now you try to kill me with the instruments I used to murder the victims of your cases. But it is a folly. I am more powerful than you."

Again, huge balls of energy hurl toward me, but his accuracy is way off. The high level of vitamin A hasn't killed him, but it has altered his power.

I give him a menacing grin as practiced as his own. "I think you know what is next."

Mr. Pierre's beady eyes narrow as I conjure a large

umbrella with a pronounced razor-sharp tip. He chuckles still not taking the situation seriously. "You are amusing, Mr. Dunne."

As I hold out the umbrella to attack, my body changes from the shifter's back to my own. Order magic has changed me back to my most powerful form.

Mr. Pierre tries to cover his alarm by hurling two huge energy balls at me. I deflect one with the umbrella, unfortunately the other hits my leg and burns through my jeans before I can knock it away. Reeling back, trying to block out the searing pain, I fight the urge to cast a numbing spell. Instead of the pain weakening me, it makes me even more determined than ever to take Mr. Pierre out once and for all.

Mr. Pierre makes several attempts to transport himself out of the bathroom. While he is distracted, I lunge forward and stab him straight through the heart with the umbrella. The transportation beam descends from the bathroom ceiling and Mr. Pierre vanishes.

I'm transported not back to Order headquarters, but back to the living room of the mansion.

Holmes sits patiently waiting and then barks loudly when he sees me materialize. "Derrick, you're alive! Thank heavens."

I reach over and hug him tight. "I have never been so happy to see your slobbering mug."

First, I catch the scent of Shalimar, then I hear Fiona's sultry voice. "I've never been happier to see your mug as well."

She races over and hugs me tight. "You were amazing. I watched the whole battle on the viewing screen at Order Headquarters. You made Mr. Hamlyn, Mr. Davis and Mr. Grump so proud tonight."

The sound of batting wings causes me to release Fiona. Another person has joined us.

Shoran stands behind Fiona. "I just wanted to thank you personally for finding the rogue shifter. While you were taking care of Mr. Pierre, I took care of the shifter."

Giving him a wry smile, I say, "That's right. I promised you the opportunity to bleed the shifter dry, didn't I?"

"You did, and Mr. Kumar made sure to have me transported to headquarters the moment the shifter was on sight."

No doubt a moment later the shifter was well on his way to death. "I'm glad we were able to work together so well. I hope you won't mind if I reach out in the future."

Shoran pats me on the back. "Of course, it would be my pleasure."

I watch as he gazes around the room, looking for a window. He doesn't need the Order's transportation beam to get back to his office. With a shrug of his shoulders, he transforms into a large brown bat.

Then I hear an unexpected voice. "I want to thank you personally for ridding WI-6 of Mr. Pierre." Mr. Bullock hands me a small silver statue picturing Hercule Poirot.

I chuckle amused that he thought Mr. Pierre

looked like the famous fictional character as well. "I'm honored, sir."

He smiles. "Good. I'd like to make you an offer to continue working for WI-6."

I stare at Mr. Bullock not sure what to say. "Can I think about it, sir?"

He nods knowing I've had quite the day. "Of course. Give me an answer by Monday."

LYING IN FIONA'S ARMS ON HER NEW BED FEELS MORE perfect than I ever imagined. I run my finger down her noble nose. "You were amazing."

She kisses my neck, then works her way up to my lips. "I thought you deserved a reward for removing Mr. Pierre from the world."

And what a reward it was. Lovemaking with Tara was like a dream but being with Fiona it feels real and in the moment. Truly fantastic.

"I hope you will consider Mr. Bullock's offer." She kisses me gently. "I love being your partner." Her hand runs down my thigh. "Also, I must admit your wizard's staff lives up to your reputation."

As if I was a schoolboy, my cheeks grow hot. Has she been talking to Krissy? My playboy days were a long time ago. Yet, the way she said it with an almost purring sound in her voice makes me want to dive back in for more. "I'm glad you approve." I kiss her deeply then come back up for air. "I can't imagine not being your partner either."

She holds the sheet around her as she jumps up out of bed. "Then it's settled. The Unusual Death Squad is ready for the next case!"

THE END

THANK YOU FROM THE AUTHOR

Thank you for reading *Death by Beer*, book one of *The Wizard Detective Derrick Dunne Series*. I appreciate you taking time out of your day to read my book. I love writing fantasies and paranormal romances and it's because of people like you that I have my dream job. I'm eternally grateful.

I sincerely hope you enjoyed reading this book as much as I enjoyed writing it. If you did, I would greatly appreciate a short review. Even just a line or two can make a huge difference. Reviews help readers discover new authors. I appreciate your support it means a lot!

ABOUT THE AUTHOR

Karin De Havin writes action-packed fantasy, and para-normal romances with kick-ass heroines who love showing villains who's boss. Writing is Karin's dream job.

Karin De Havin is known for her unique books that explore celestial worlds, time travel with a Victorian genie, follow the life of a human chameleon, attend the Genie Academy class of 1890, and travel to Tokyo and learn that ghosts are real.

Find out more about her books at her website www.karindehavin.com.

Join Karin's newsletter for book inspired recipes in the *Baking with Books* segment and receive a free short story!

Click here to join Karin's newsletter!

www.ingramcontent.com/pod-product-compliance
Lightning Source LLC
Chambersburg PA
CBHW021438150726
47989CB00001B/289